"You Actually Want To Reopen The Old Feud. You Want Revenge."

It was to Celine's benefit that Tyrell knew this was not a whim, but a need that drove her every breath. "You got it, buddy."

"Well, then," he said slowly. He stretched slowly, and Celine blinked at all that male body rippling in front of her. She swallowed abruptly as an unfamiliar little feminine lurch that she couldn't define stabbed at her. Celine liked everything in black and white; she did not like unsteady emotions.

Tyrell's slow smile might have devastated another woman. "I guess you've got to deal with me, then. I appreciate the notice. And thanks for referring to me earlier as a 'big, juicy tomato.' I'm honored, and you've gone to all this trouble, too, to pick me from my vine. My, that makes me feel so special."

Tyrell Blaylock, the man she'd ruined, was flirting with her!

Dear Reader,

Merry Christmas from Silhouette Desire—where you're guaranteed powerful, passionate and provocative love stories that feature rugged heroes and spirited heroines who experience the full emotional intensity of falling in love!

The always-wonderful Cait London is back with this December's MAN OF THE MONTH, who happens to be one of THE BLAYLOCKS. In *Typical Male,* a modern warrior hero is attracted to the woman who wants to destroy him.

The thrilling Desire miniseries TEXAS CATTLEMAN'S CLUB concludes with *Lone Star Prince* by Cindy Gerard. Her Royal Princess Anna von Oberland finally reunites with the dashing attorney Gregory Hunt who fathered her child years ago.

Talented Ashley Summers returns to Desire with *That Loving Touch,* where a pregnant woman becomes snowbound with a sexy executive in his cabin. The ever-popular BACHELOR BATTALION gets into the holiday spirit with *Marine under the Mistletoe* by Maureen Child. *Star-Crossed Lovers* is a Romeo-and-Juliet-with-a-happy-ending story by Zena Valentine. And an honorable cowboy demands the woman pregnant with his child marry him in Christy Lockhart's *The Cowboy's Christmas Baby.*

Each and every month, Silhouette Desire offers you six exhilarating journeys into the seductive world of romance. So make a commitment to sensual love and treat yourself to all six for some great holiday reading this month!

Enjoy!

Joan Marlow Golan
Senior Editor, Silhouette Desire

Please address questions and book requests to:
Silhouette Reader Service
U.S.: 3010 Walden Ave., P.O. Box 1325, Buffalo, NY 14269
Canadian: P.O. Box 609, Fort Erie, Ont. L2A 5X3

Typical Male
CAIT LONDON

Published by Silhouette Books
America's Publisher of Contemporary Romance

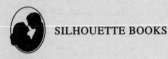 **SILHOUETTE BOOKS**

ISBN 0-373-76255-0

TYPICAL MALE

Visit us at www.romance.net

Printed in U.S.A.

Books by Cait London

CAIT LONDON

lives in the Missouri Ozarks but loves to travel the Northwest's gold rush/cattle drive trails every summer. She enjoys research trips, meeting people and going to Native American dances. Ms. London is an avid reader who loves to paint, play with computers and grow herbs (particularly scented geraniums right now). She's a national bestselling and award-winning author, and she has also written historical romances under another pseudonym. Three is her lucky number; she has three daughters, and the events in her life have always been in threes. "I love writing for Silhouette," Cait says. "One of the best perks about all this hard work is the thrilling reader response and the warm, snug sense that I have given readers an enjoyable, entertaining gift."

For my daughter Karla

One

"**A** woman, and she looks like trouble." Tyrell leaned back into the shadows of Wyoming's Rocky Mountain pines and firs and studied the woman marching up the rugged path to his cabin hideaway. Her stride wasn't easy, but firm, with a purpose—she wanted something.

His ex-fiancée had used other methods. But his sister, Else, the matron of the extensive Blaylock family, walked like that, and she always had a purpose.

Tyrell wiped the sweat from his chin with his forearm. Chopping wood took away a measure of his dark mood. He traced the zigzagging route of a red fox in the brush, then scanned the cloudy sky where a golden eagle seemed to hover in the high winds. At this altitude, late May was cold, though the ranches below were decked in spring's vivid green. Six months ago, he had been a top executive, a chief of finance for a New York corporate office. Now the only peace he'd found was about to be invaded by a woman.

He wasn't in a mood to deal with anyone, even his family. Else didn't like her brothers to escape her. James, Logan, Dan, Roman and Rio all had wives and only lightly mourned the freedom of "holing-up."

Until Tyrell had settled the storms within him, he was doing just that, taking a "breather" and coming home to the source of his peace—the mountains and his family.

He hefted the ax and placed his thoughts in numerical order. He liked numbers; they had always served him well. He swung the ax at the trunk of the tree and began to count his thoughts with each solid whack. One—when he'd found what he needed, settled that savage edge riding him, then he would— He swung the ax again, coming down on the first cut to create a wedge that would eventually fell the tree. Two—go in for the kill, find out who started the rumors about him. Someone had been tracking his life, his credit cards, his bank account, his methods of travel and telephone bills. Three—the ax bit into the wood with an expert cut that would eventually topple it. Returning home was all part of his plan to sort out his life. *And it would be a long time before he'd trust a woman.*

A hawk, seeking a mouse, soared in the clear blue Wyoming sky as Tyrell gripped his ax tightly. The woman continued her steady march toward his sanctuary. The few women in Tyrell's life had always wanted something—cash, career, status. At one time, he'd wanted those things, too. Now he didn't; he wanted peace. Tyrell's gaze swept over Jasmine, the small Wyoming town nestled in the valley below. His ancestor Micah Blaylock had settled the valley and had taken a bride, and the Blaylock name was rich with honor and respect. The youngest of seven children, Tyrell had come home again to find that honor and family values he'd tossed away the years he'd worked to build Mason Diversified. Mason's, a top shipping and label company, now owned many subsidiary companies with varied interests, but Tyrell had paid a dear price. He'd been away from his family and his roots too long.

Micah Blaylock's old cabin had been Tyrell's refuge—rebuilding it had given him what he'd needed.

It wasn't easy to move back into his family. He couldn't forget his father's last telephone call—Tyrell should have come home and didn't. He'd been too busy chalking up profits for Mason Diversified.

He inhaled the fresh morning air, scented of spring. Soon there would be wild roses beginning to bud. A mountain blue bird shot across the sky, and new leaves shimmered on the cottonwood trees. And the air around him simmered with regrets. Now his parents were gone, killed in an accident on icy roads. He wondered if that ice had shrouded his heart, pictures of their crushed car in the deep canyon haunting him.

He studied the woman invading his peace. Then, with a curse, he expertly threw the ax he'd been using to cut wood; the ax handle rotated once in midair, the steel sinking deep into the trunk of an aspen tree. "If she makes it past that old rock slide, it will take her about two hours to get to the meadow, and she's not getting past that. I came up here for peace and quiet."

The woman, dressed in a ball cap, a dull red sweater against the morning chill and khaki shorts, placed one hand on a boulder and vaulted over it. Her small round glasses glinted, washed by the cloudy morning sun as she leaped over a stream and continued steadily upward on the rocky path. In a direct as-the-crow-flies line, she was not far from Tyrell's cabin; however, the winding trail around a small canyon added to the walking time. From his high vantage point, Tyrell noticed her hiking boots and the slender athletic legs above them. Her backpack shifted as she vaulted over a log.

"She'll sprain something and I'll be stuck with her." Tyrell had had enough of women for a long time. Hillary had left deep bruises. His ex-fiancée, the daughter of his boss, wasn't exactly the love of his life, but she suited Tyrell's rising financial career. After a five-year relationship, he'd expected her to believe his word against the rumor mongers'. His jaw tightened beneath his two-week beard. *Someone had set out to deliberately sabotage his career, starting rumors about his private life and making insinuations about selling Mason Diversified's lucrative client list to competitors.*

An aging playboy, and jealous of Tyrell's youth and fitness, Melvin Mason had gradually grown to resent his top man on a personal basis. Mason wanted singular control of the company, now that the firm was showing high profit.

Descended from hunters, Tyrell's eyes jerked to a bighorn sheep, leaping on the red rock cliff above the cabin. Tyrell had expected his future father-in-law and employer of the past ten years to believe him. Insecure, feeling threatened and looking for reasons to strip Tyrell's growing control of the company, Melvin Mason had believed what he wanted and took the rumors as truth. Melvin wasn't the understanding sort, but then Tyrell hadn't asked for friendship. He'd pushed Mason Diversified into a sleek, high profit company and had made millions for Mason. Tyrell liked numbers lining up to make neat profit. His colleagues hadn't questioned his integrity; they respected him. He'd expected the same from his fiancée and an employer whom he had made rich. He hadn't asked Hillary or her father for warmth; he'd asked them to believe him. After years of association, he hadn't doubted that they would give him time to root out the troublemaker.

They hadn't. Without waiting, without questioning or letting Tyrell untangle the gossip, Mason had wanted the company to himself. He wanted to play power hardball, ripping away Tyrell's position and employee benefits. A bad move on Mason's part—the aftershocks included Mason's top clients calling Tyrell and asking for referrals to Mason's competitors.

After Hillary's and Mason's reactions to the rumors that Tyrell had a sleazy private life, he hadn't cared who started the trouble; he'd had enough after a long series of Mason's attempts to undermine him. Prior to the final break, the day Mason ordered him out of the building, Tyrell's instinct told him there was trouble. Two weeks before that day, Tyrell had moved to protect the investments and retirement portfolios of his staff and fellow workers, who wanted him to fight and who believed in him. Then, when their investments were safe and established in accounts outside Mason's reach, Tyrell had set to work destroying what he'd built. On that final day, one touch of his finger to just one computer key, set into action damage that could not be repaired.

Descended from Apaches and Spanish conquistadors with a mix of European settler thrown in, Tyrell knew how to fight. He knew how to streamline profits and he knew how to fatten loss. He left Mason with a shell of a company, the same as it was ten years ago. Then he'd walked away, sickened by the lifestyle he had once wanted.

To mend, he'd come back to Jasmine, Wyoming, and his family, the Blaylocks. He'd sort out his disappointment and anger, in himself and in Mason, and then he'd rebuild his life.

Startled by his sudden flash of temper, Tyrell rhythmically slapped his thigh. Damn it, he wanted privacy, not visitors and chitchat or a helpless woman underfoot. The woman walked across a fallen log bridging another creek and Tyrell held his breath, hoping she wouldn't fall. Instead she sat on a gray boulder and drew off her ball cap. Short, vibrant strawberry-red curls gleamed in the dim gray morning, her face small and pale in the distance.

"She'll sunburn in this high mountain sun, even though it is cloudy." Tyrell narrowed his eyes as she removed something from her backpack, stripped off her glasses and began rubbing her face and legs. "So she knows about sun protection, but there's a whole lot more up here that can make life hard on a woman, including me. She's not getting past my meadow."

He glanced at the clouds and mist swirling around the black-rock jagged mountain above him. This was his element now, where he could trim his dark savage temper chopping wood and adding onto his log cabin. Rain was not far away, the air was heavy, fragrant with dampness. When the rain began, she'd change her mind and start back after resting. Then he could return to the peace he had to have....

"I want him to see me coming. I want him to know that I am Cutter Lomax's granddaughter and that I'm taking away his family homestead." Celine Lomax smiled tightly, coldly. After a full year of working to destroy Tyrell Blaylock, she was closing in to take away the Blaylock land. She'd spent her entire savings to finance recouping the land that was her birthright, according to her grandfather, Cutter Lomax. She knew his flaws, but they hadn't stopped her love of him. Perhaps it was Cutter's strength; her father and his son, Link, had been a much weaker man who failed at everything. Perhaps it was his expression when he talked about the land that had been taken from him. Or perhaps she'd always fought for the underdog, and Cutter's lost claim appealed to that element of her nature. She, who had only two men for relatives, had held them close and dear, despite their flaws. Whatever the reason, *she believed her deceased grandfather, without question.*

As a surveyor, she had the skill to demolish the Blaylock claim to land Cutter Lomax said was rightfully his. She'd built her life, chosen her career, for this moment. Cutter's revenge had been passed on to his son, Celine's father, and she'd teethed on revenge. Now it was hers to carry out.

The unmarried, pampered, playboy baby of the Blaylocks was the perfect starting point.

Today, she was edgy, tired and riding on nerves and coffee. For years, she'd worked overtime in freezing sleet, snow higher than her head and egg-frying temperatures. She'd hoarded every penny to finance tearing down the Blaylocks and their friend Boone Llewlyn. Except for long silk thermal underwear that was worth the high price, her wardrobe ran to anything she could wad into a duffel bag and wash in an icy creek. If she needed more, she stopped in a thrift shop along the way.

Light rain began and mist layered the meadow ahead of her. She shifted her aching shoulders under the heavy backpack that contained everything she owned. She'd paid her father and grandfather's medical bills and spared nothing for herself. She'd teethed on "taking down the Blaylocks," a phrase repeated by both men and now she was primed for action.

Raindrops fell from the shimmering aspens, dampening her clothing. She inhaled the mist, loving it. She preferred to work outdoors, rather than in an office. Her jacket was in her backpack; she should have been cold, but her fast march and her dark mood kept her warm. Celine was halfway across the alpine meadow, lush with mountain grass and gleaming with dew, when she saw him.

She gripped a damp stalk and tore it from the fragrant mountain earth. Through the layers of rain and mist, she recognized Tyrell Blaylock from the photograph she'd taken of him waiting for a New York taxi. He'd had the lean look of a predator, narrowed black eyes, taut jaw and a mouth that looked as if it had been cut into stone. This man's face was just as hard and hawkish, bones thrusting against his dark skin, though on that New York city sidewalk he had been dressed in a designer shirt and tie, and an expensive pin-striped suit.

Now rain shimmered on his body and he had that same alert, impatient hawkish look. Cutter had said that the Blaylocks resembled their Apache and Spanish conquistadors' ancestors, that they were a dark, gleaming, powerfully-built family. Cutter had said you could tell a Blaylock by their "Spanish eyes"— expressive eyes—and now this tall, rangy man's were spearing her.

Unnoticed by him, she'd studied him six months ago. She'd expected Tyrell Blaylock's straight, gleaming, blue-black Native American hair to be neatly, expensively clipped. She hadn't expected the heavy shoulder-length cut to be pushed back from his hard-boned face with a sweaty red bandanna headband. The twin narrow braids framing his face added to the savage look.

She hadn't expected the sweat gleaming on the dark skin of his bare chest, and his taut, powerful arms. His muscles rippled across his body as he walked smoothly toward her. She jumped when a taut muscle on his chest contracted suddenly, the dark nipple shifting on the smooth, gleaming surface. Celine blinked. An expensive gym-pampered body was smooth, but the ridges shifting under Tyrell Blaylock's darkly tanned skin were those of a workman, more defined, edgy, taut. Wearing only his worn jeans and the red bandanna tied over his forehead, Tyrell could have emerged from the West a century ago. The long knife sheathed at his waist did not soften his appearance.

When he stood near her, Celine fought a shiver. His worn moccasins were locked to the spring earth, long hard legs braced wide, and his arms crossed over his chest in a forbidding pose. Tyrell Blaylock, up close and away from his city veneer, towered over her five-foot-six height. And there was nothing friendly in his black, searing eyes. Maybe she'd gone too far, maybe she'd pushed Tyrell over the edge.... How would he react when she told him…? She couldn't worry about Tyrell's sensitivity; she'd come too far, committed too much to his destruction. "I'm Celine Lomax and you are Tyrell Blaylock, lately of New York and Mason Diversified. We've never met. Spare me the 'how do you do's.'"

His black brows scowled down at her, and Celine braced herself for what she had promised Cutter and her father she'd do—take away Blaylock land. Cutter had blamed Luke Blaylock, Tyrell's grandfather, for gaining the affections of Garnet, the woman he wanted. He'd blamed Boone Llewlyn for thwarting his real estate plans; he'd blamed them both for ruining his life and fortune. He'd blamed Celine for being female instead of the grandson who could reclaim his land, and Cutter had died a bitter man. "I see you recognize the name. Cutter Lomax was my grandfather. I've come to survey and make good my grandfather's claim on what is now Blaylock land. Don't worry. I don't intend to take the whole Blaylock and Llewlyn land, but I am reclaiming Cutter Lomax's honor and *his* land. You've heard of Cutter Lomax, of course. He is a legend in this country. The Blaylocks and Boone Llewlyn were afraid of him. That's why they ruined him."

"How did you know about New York and Mason Diversified?" His words were clipped, deep and laden with warning, each one hitting her like lightning bolts. Those black eyes slowly took in her worn sweater, her ragged cutoff khaki pants and her worn hiking boots, topped by thick socks.

Celine lifted her head. She didn't need dresses or New York designer labels; she had money enough to do what she had to do. She'd have to work while ferreting out the truth, but she'd always worked, keeping house for Cutter and her father for as long as she could remember. They'd said her mother didn't love her; that she hadn't cared enough to stay. Celine had Cutter and her father, and then they were gone after years of drinking and mourning their loss to the Blaylocks.

Their revenge had become hers; their anger at the Blaylocks was one of her first memories. She'd come this far and now she pushed out the words she'd been savoring, shafting them at him. "You're licking your bruises, Blaylock, and I'm the one who gave them to you. You won't be dissecting struggling little mail-order companies anymore and shoving them into Mason Diversified's hungry jaws. You won't be boxing in and buying shares for takeovers anymore. But hey, maybe you could work in one of their label factories—packing shipping boxes or something. Let's see—they were a label company until you moved in. Then they became international, and with your calculator for brains, they started grasping struggling little companies. They had to ship those mail-order products, so you watched for a sinking company and moved in for the kill. You revamped Mason's financial structure and employee benefits, and streamlined operations. I can see why Mason believed everything. As chief financial officer, you knew too much, had too much control and powerful friends, and you posed a threat to him.''

His gaze ripped down her body, then jarred as it locked with hers. ''Lomax,'' he said flatly, as if the word stood for trouble.

''You got it, Blaylock. The name is Lomax. The company I was working for sent me to do the survey on a building and parking lot for Mason Diversified's in Montana. I caught the name on the contract and dug out a few facts, like Jasmine, Wyoming, home of the Blaylocks, who my grandfather said stole away his life. He hated the Blaylocks and Boone Llewlyn and for good reason. He died penniless and so did my father, and I paid their bills. They should have had an easier life…thanks to the Blaylocks and that land-grabber Boone Llewlyn, they didn't. It wasn't hard to follow your trail back to corporate headquarters in New York, and guess what? There was the baby of the Blaylocks, right in my sight.''

''You…are the woman who 'accidentally' bumped into my fian—to Hillary Mason in a shopping mall and said that you were pregnant with my child? That we had a toddler at home and you were destitute because I wasn't providing for you?'' The words were carefully placed, echoing loudly when Tyrell's voice was deep and soft, too soft.

Celine forced a cheerful smile. That hit-and-run disguise had worked; they'd never find the woman again. His frown deepened. ''You're the woman who sent the thank-you letter to Mason. You said that I'd sold his private client list to you, contact information that was vital to sales and promotion of products?''

''I was proud of that letter. A few chats with employees who think Mason is insecure and jealous of you, and I was off to the races. I told Mason that I thought it was very nice of him to allow you to sell a 'best client' list to a competitor.''

"Mason was too furious and eager to get me out to check on that. You are, of course, the same woman who again bumped into Hillary at the doorway of Mason Diversified Corporate Building. But this time you were dressed in a leopard skin bodysuit and six-inch heels and wearing a long blond wig and fake eyelashes. You asked the way to my office to perform the services I had requested at noon? You hoped you wouldn't get that much oil on my desk this time?" His eyes drifted down her compact, athletic body and her worn clothing.

The leopard-seductress image didn't fit her now; she'd played the part to perfection and even enjoyed dressing up as a femme fatale. The seductress-for-one-day could never be traced. Celine allowed her smile to grow. "I was on rest and relaxation leave from my company. New York seemed to be the place to visit. Your ex-fiancée was shocked. Especially when I told her that all of my 'working' girlfriends knew and liked you."

"Exactly how did you get your information about me?" His question was like a whip cracking the cold, misty air.

"Your secretary is such a motherly woman. We had a chat in the ladies' room. That day, I was the scrub woman down on my luck." She almost felt guilty. When she'd begun sobbing, Mary's arms had enclosed her like a mother's. But Celine didn't know about a mother's arms, and she had a job to do—get revenge.

"You took advantage of Mary's soft heart. That wasn't nice, Lomax. You realize that you can get into legal trouble for damaging my reputation and career. You wouldn't like the penalties. Why would you admit this now? To me?"

"I wondered when you'd get to that. You won't raise a fuss. You'll protect your family and your reputation—what's left of it. You won't want anyone knowing that the Blaylocks and Llewlyn were land grabbers. It's all so simple, Blaylock. I want you to see me coming. I knew you'd run back here to lick your bruises—"

One black eyebrow lifted, challenging her; the morning air sizzled with electricity. Tyrell's gaze drifted lazily over her face. "Lick my bruises? *Run* back here?" he repeated slowly, the sound was that of a wolf growling low in its throat just before he—

She'd been threatened before; it was her earliest memory. "You're here, aren't you? And not cuddled up to Hillary-poo?"

"Let's keep on track, Lomax. Why did you choose me? I've got a big family."

"You're the baby, Blaylock. The soft spot of the family. Five brothers and one sister and they all dote on you. You were prime for the picking, like a big juicy tomato. I checked out your career and reputation and then I studied you. There you were, standing on that street corner, waiting for a taxi. You fairly dripped in expensive designer labels, you checked time on a wristwatch that cost more than some cars. And you just had that spoiled, pampered city-boy look."

She took a breath. "I just didn't like you when I saw you. I didn't care if my tactics worked. I was coming to Jasmine anyway to survey *Lomax* land, but taking you down—you know, a Lomax taking down a Blaylock, was just something I had to try. I had time off, and pushing a Blaylock out of his cushy job seemed right. If your fiancée and your boss hadn't believed me, that was just fine, too. But it was worth the effort, and it paid off, didn't it?"

Anger boiled out of her as she drove home the spear. Tyrell Blaylock had everything and an easy life road; she'd had to scrimp and work for every penny. He'd zipped through college on academic and athletic scholarships; she'd had to care for her sick grandfather and father and work for grocery money, and provide for them. They were all she had—they said her mother had run off when she was only a year old. She hadn't had time to date, but finally, as a teenager, she reached for romance. What she found was brief, painful sex in the back seat of a car.

She studied his tall angular body. A man with Tyrell's looks would have found everything so easy, including sex; she resented that, too. "You were looking at a solid-gold future with the Masons. I wanted to ruin you just as your grandfather and his friend Boone ruined my grandfather. So I gave you a few well-picked Christmas presents and you went down."

"That's called stalking, Lomax. I could stop everything with one phone call to the police, but I won't. I'm going to enjoy the look on your face when you find out that the land has always been Blaylock." Tyrell's expression shifted slightly, the corner of his mouth quirking as though he was restraining a grin. He reached to run his thumb along her cheek. "A drop of sun lotion you didn't rub in when you stopped to eat that sandwich," he explained.

He'd been watching her. Just as she had watched him. A slight cold chill lifted the hair on her nape. Men just did not watch her; she was part of a work crew—a brief passing glance during a poker game was tops and that was to see if she was bluffing. Now, Tyrell Blaylock was dissecting her piece by piece. Celine inhaled and locked herself to what she had to do; she couldn't be derailed by him searching out every freckle on her face, by studying her green eyes…well, one did have that spot of brown. She fought the shiver that lifted the hair on her nape; she hadn't been studied that close—ever. She brushed away the thought that Tyrell was looking at her as a prospective sensual encounter. Men considered her as one of the boys.

She tried to ignore his slow gaze traveling over her cropped reddish-blond curls. She jerked her head to one side as he plucked a leaf from her hair and showed it to her, his eyebrows lifting innocently. She really did not like that slight curve to his mouth, just that bit of lift that said he wasn't taking her seriously. He would…once she dug out old abstracts, journals and anything else she could find to prove her case. "You're only thirty-seven, Blaylock. You can build a new career. You're just—"

She released a smirk and eyed him. "You're just taking a time-out now, and everyone knows you're too high powered for this little burg. I saw you there in New York and you looked just exactly like my grandfather said Luke Blaylock looked, like 'the lord of the land.' I knew you were the perfect place to begin. I checked you out. You like numbers and take-overs. You won scholarships and aced college, the whole bit. You're very smart. The braids are a nice touch, by the way. If you're trying for a warrior effect. A city boy playing at macho games—my, my."

His smile was tight and chilling. "Thank you for that much. You're half my size, you're on *my* mountain, and you're calling me out—threatening me and my family. I suppose you're also the woman who called Diversified's switchboard. You left a message for me to bring a can of whipped cream, my Tarzan loincloth and lots of scented oil for our date at that sleazy hotel? It was a bit overkill, wasn't it?"

She'd really put everything she had into that scenario. Pushing away a smirk, she blinked up at him innocently. "Oh, dear. Did I leave that message for Mason to give to you? How silly of me. And my size hasn't got anything to do with—"

"And you've got a fast mouth." Those black eyes dipped quickly to her mouth, searing it, then jerked back up to lock with her eyes. "You're going to need much more than threats to deal with me or take any portion of my family's land away. Tell me why you think you have claim to my family land."

She lifted her chin, glaring up at him. Raindrops dripped steadily from the brim of her ball cap. She inched to the left to avoid the steady drip coming from the aspen limbs above her. "My grandfather said so."

He lifted those black eyebrows and reached to switch her cap backward, revealing her face. His dark narrowed gaze sliced at her. "And that's it?"

Celine jerked her ball cap visor around to shield her expression. One remark about her freckles or her family and she'd—
"It's enough. He wouldn't lie. He told me the whole story, again and again. It never changed— He bought several pieces of property and he had a deed, the boundaries marked. He had a good house in a high mountain canyon and he was just getting a good start in ranching when your grandfather and Boone decided they wanted the land. They said it was Blaylock and Llewlyn land and that he had no right to it. They said that he'd bought a small piece of property by threatening the owners and then had moved the boundary markers on their land. Then Luke Blaylock, your grandfather and sheriff at the time, kept after him and he couldn't work to pay the lawyers. The judge who sent him to prison on various robbery charges and assault was bought somehow, or the witnesses were. Then the Blaylocks got the land."

Celine sucked in air, her temper raging. "I'm a surveyor, Blaylock, and a good one. I know how to read courthouse records, abstracts, and dig at the truth. If a rebar—a metal boundary marker—has been moved one inch, I'll know. If a pile of rocks serving as a boundary in pioneer times has been moved, I'll know. If a stone marker has been sandblasted to erase the chiseled inscription, I'll know." She narrowed her eyes behind her round tinted glasses and leveled a stare at him. She hoped the raindrops and steam on her lenses wouldn't diminish the impact of her threat. "I'm especially good at forged deeds. I chose my career with just this moment in mind—to bring down the Blaylocks."

Celine forced herself not to move as Tyrell lazily reached out a big hand. He lifted her ball cap and eased a finger through her jumble of curls. She forced herself to stand still; she wouldn't be intimidated by his size. Celine fought a shiver as Tyrell said slowly, "Let me get this straight. You're dedicated to proving your grandfather's...belief was the truth."

He was toying with her hair, winding it around his finger,

studying the strands, and not taking her seriously. If there was
one thing that could set off her Lomax temper, it was a man
taking her too lightly. Celine wished he hadn't seen her hands
curl into fists; the quick glint of satisfaction in his eyes said he
had. She grabbed her ball cap and jerked it down on her head.
"Cutter Lomax would not lie to me. Those boundary markers
were moved, and he did not commit robbery. The sheriff, your
grandfather, sent an innocent man to jail and then took his
land!''

Tyrell's lazy gaze lowered to study her expression. She hated
her own intensity and wished she were more skilled at covering
her emotions—she wasn't; she had never played games. He
spoke slowly, "You're serious about this. You actually want
to reopen Cutter's old feud. You want revenge."

She pounced on the words, "feud" and "revenge." It was
to her benefit that Tyrell knew this was not a whim, but a need
that drove her every breath. "You got it, buddy."

"Well, then," he said slowly. He stretched slowly and traced
a deer moving through the woods. Celine blinked at all that
male body rippling in front of her. Working in the field, she'd
seen men without shirts, but they were just—she swallowed
abruptly as an unfamiliar need stabbed at her. Just a feminine
little lurch that she couldn't define. Celine liked everything in
black-and-white descriptions, surveyed in neat definite lines
with boundary markers; she did not like unsteady emotions.

Tyrell's slow smile might have devastated another woman.
"I guess you've got to deal with me. I appreciate the notice.
And thanks for referring to me as a 'big juicy tomato.' I'm
honored, and you've gone to all this trouble, too, to pick me
from my vine. My, that makes me feel so special."

She nodded grimly, satisfied that Tyrell was taking her as a
serious threat. Then the notion struck her that Tyrell Blaylock,
the man she'd ruined, was flirting with her. Uncertain, she eyed
him through her steamy glasses. Only men desperate for
women in her remote work sites had ever made passes at her.

She'd squashed those ideas without hesitation. For the most part, the men she knew considered her efficient, precise and one of the boys.

A man, not one of the boys, stood in front of her, towering over her. Tyrell Blaylock was sleek, hard and unshaken by her threat. She eyed him; maybe he had a dual personality and could flip back at any moment to his sleek city-hunter image. Either way, she had him tacked to the wall and she wasn't backing off.

His high cheekbones gleamed, a muscle moving rhythmically in his jaw. "Let's just keep this between us, shall we, Lomax?"

"You're already bargaining, Blaylock. That makes me happy. I've got you worried and that's a good sign."

He lifted that disbelieving eyebrow again. "You could be wrong. All you have is your grandfather's side of the story."

"I'm not wrong. But I agree that it would make my research easier if your family and neighbors didn't worry about protecting their land. After I get the information I need, I'll turn my case over to an attorney. Or your family can pay me for the land and we'll assess damages, starting with all the medical bills of my grandfather and father." Her stomach twisted painfully. The markers over their graves were the cheapest— She looked away from Tyrell, stiff with pain in her body and her mind.

"Do you agree that the rest of my family won't enter this?" Tyrell asked slowly, defining the ground rules and pushing her.

She hated being pushed. She waited because she knew he wanted an answer, and she wasn't ready to give it to him. "Hey. I'm setting the ground rules. I'm the one with a plan. I'm in control of this gig, got it? This isn't a fancy boardroom. I'm not obligated to you."

"You are if you want to stay out of jail and work as a surveyor again. I'm happy to play your little busybody game—"

She turned on him, burning with fury. She could have leaped upon him and— "'Busybody game'?"

He lowered his head, meeting her glare. His fist gripped her sweater to draw her up on the tip of her toes. "You've got a temper, Lomax. You push my family and I'll call in a few favors. I didn't leave corporate America because I was forced out. I had job offers and colleagues who would have stood with me. I walked."

"That's a lie. I ruined you. Me…a Lomax, and you're not blackmailing me. I don't go down easy. You're living up here in a cabin because you're broke and hiding out. High wheelers and dealers can lose it as easy as they make it. Or maybe it's just good old shame that you've been kicked out."

"'A lie,'" he repeated slowly, dangerously, as if no one had ever dared speak to him like that. The vein in his throat stood out in relief. He hitched her a fraction higher, his breath sweeping across her face as their stares locked. "I'll bet that backpack is heavy," he said slowly.

"Not a bit," she lied, though the straps would probably leave chafe marks. Her tiptoes barely touched the ground, but she wasn't frightened. If Blaylock wanted to test her, that was fine. She'd lived with bullies all her life. "I've walked across deserts carrying this weight and more."

His eyes darkened and shot down to her mouth. She licked her lips and hoped she didn't have a crumb of that last cookie on them—that would ruin her going-for-the-kill image.

"You like gingersnap cookies, do you, Lomax?" he asked in a tone that sent a jolt of electricity to every tense muscle in her body. There was just a hint of play, of curiosity, and something darker, deeper, more elemental.

Celine tensed. Whatever the ball game was right now, she didn't know how to play. Tethered by his grip, she glared at him. In her lifetime, when uncertain, she'd found that glaring was always a safe defensive move. Tyrell's eyes narrowed, pinning her. The air seemed to slither, tingle and heat as if it were alive; it sucked away her breath, and sent tiny thunderbolts through her body. That uncertain churning in her stomach had to be too little sleep and too much coffee. She pushed away the unfamiliar tense emotion and went for a solid jab on what she suspected might be a tender spot. "When Papa jerked your position, she didn't want a working man. Hillary-poo chose not to believe you, didn't she? And then she couldn't leave Papa's money for someone who is down and out, could she?"

His expression darkened, tightened and then he abruptly released her sweater. He rubbed his jaw and the sound of beard against his rough palm echoed eerily in the misty air. "Has anyone ever told you that you're not exactly sweet?"

"You're hurting my feelings, Blaylock," she shot at him cheerfully. She blew away the raindrop that had been clinging to the end of her nose.

His expression softened, humor dancing in his black eyes. "You're wet clear through, Lomax. A pitiful soggy little thing."

She snorted at the "little thing." She'd worked right beside her crew, blazing heat and freezing ice storms. She'd hauled wood for campfires, climbed mountains and— "At least I'm dressed, not standing half-naked in a drenching rain and playing at being a mountain man."

Tyrell looked slowly down her body and Celine realized that her flesh had chilled, her nipples thrusting against the damp sweater. She usually wore a vest in the cold, but men's chests did the same thing in cold weather. She was sturdily built, probably a gift from her Scots-Irish ancestors. She watched, fascinated as a dark flush rose up his cheeks. He closed his eyes, groaned and turned, striding through the wet grass away from her.

"Hey! I'm not done with you," she shouted, trudging after him through the sodden meadow. "You haven't heard all the good stuff yet. You're just a typical male, you know…running when things get tough."

He turned his head to glower at her over his shoulder, then turned and kept walking.

"Running, huh?" she called, enjoying herself for the first time in—in forever. Her grin stopped when he allowed a small wet branch to flip back in her face. She sputtered, mopping the water from her face as she hurried after him. "You did that on purpose. I should have expected something sneaky like that from a Blaylock."

Her backpack slipped and as she struggled to tug it back up again, her glasses went awry. Tyrell appeared out of the mist and stripped the backpack away. Dangling from his large hand, it looked like a toy. With his other hand, he straightened her glasses. "Coming, dear?" he asked between his teeth. "Or don't you know enough to get out of the rain?"

Celine tensed, leaning toward him, her fists at her side. Tyrell's mouth jerked as though he were hiding a grin. She wouldn't tolerate anyone making fun of her. "Are you calling me a 'twit'?"

"If the name fits—" Tyrell easily blocked the fist she shot at his stomach. Without missing a heartbeat, he slid her glasses from her and pushed them into her hand. "Here. Hold these."

Then he bent and scooped her over his shoulder and began loping easily through the forest. He carried her over the narrow path as if she were a child.

Tyrell jerked open his cabin door and eased through it, carrying his squirming burden. That compact, squirming body had muscles, and Celine knew how to swear. Just what he would expect from Cutter Lomax's granddaughter.

She was stubborn, willful, hot-tempered, and he felt a warm glow just looking at her. As he looked down at her in the rain-drenched meadow he wasn't happy about the odd light-hearted feeling curling around him. Bristling, threatening him and his family, and scented of gingersnap cookies, rain and mist, she was loyal and untouched— *Untouched*. Every male instinct he had told him that Celine was an innocent. Defenseless, alone and fiercely defending her grandfather's lies as truth, Celine Lomax hadn't a clue that he'd found her interesting—as a woman.

Two

In Micah Blaylock's refinished log cabin, Tyrell knew how his ancestor must have felt, wanting to claim his reluctant bride. The thought shocked him; he had streamlined his life and wasn't prepared for elemental emotions for a woman.

Tyrell fought a groan. He'd just escaped a cold, empty life with Hillary Mason. The last thing he needed to do now was to stand in a Rocky Mountain meadow, watch Celine's soft, sweet mouth hurl threats at him and notice that she was all woman. That she was firm, soft in the right places and had hair that magically, silkily curled around his finger, ensnaring and delighting him. The same color as her lashes, the strands seemed to sparkle in the cloudy day, the varied sun-lightened shades warming his fingers. He'd wanted to run a fingertip across her lashes, those long softly bristling lashes with sparks flashing at the tips, and those freckles. He'd wondered if they danced on the rest of that milky skin.... If a grown man could swoon, he almost did when she'd smirked. Those flashing green eyes turned sultry, darkening. An intoxicating little dimple had played on her left cheek; he'd begun to wonder how it would feel beneath his fingertips and how her bottom would feel cupped in his hands.

Celine Lomax's bottom. It was now propped over his shoulder. He glanced at his hand, open and splayed, possessively digging in on her bottom. The soft flowing surface burned his palm. He frowned and forced his fingers to straighten, his palm rigid and flat. He lifted his hand slightly away. She'd ruined his career; she should be hauled into court and—

She believed Cutter Lomax; she wouldn't believe anything else until Cutter's lies were proven wrong. Cutter's reputation for land fraud, shakedown and other money-making schemes was legendary. Tyrell's grandfather, Luke Blaylock, had gained a scar from Cutter's blade; he'd tried to stop Cutter from mistreating a worn-out horse.

She'd stopped screaming and wiggling. She was using the limp, deadweight method to wear him down. Tyrell hefted Celine from his shoulder and plopped her into a chair. Her body balled as if to hurl herself at him. Celine's furious green eyes dominated her pale face, her mouth pressed into a tight line. Under her ball cap, which was on sideways, her curls seemed to explode, fiery red around her face. One dainty ear was framed in her curls. It was a delectable ear, unpierced and sweet. A virgin ear. He wanted to nibble on it.

Every muscle in his body flexed; goose bumps rode his body. Instincts he'd hidden from the world shot him a solid thump, low in his stomach. He breathed uneasily, shaken by the need to take her to his bed. In the small one room, he caught her scent and hoped his nostrils didn't quiver, inhaling every nuance. She smelled like rain on a tender rosebud as yet unfurled—sweet, tight and exciting to explore.

Tyrell did not want to explore Celine Lomax; he wanted her out of his life. He shoved the backpack no woman her size ought to be carrying into her hands. He ran his hands down his wet face, plucked off her ball cap and tossed a dry towel over her head. "It's raining sheets out there. The creeks will be swollen by now and—''

She hadn't moved, the towel remained draped over her head. Rain ran down her bare legs and a pool of water formed around her worn boots. Tyrell studied her as he swept another towel over his head, chest and arms. He hurled it and the wet bandanna from his forehead into a corner and watched her, his hands braced on his hips.

He wanted to kick off his sodden moccasins. But Cindi, his brother Roman's adopted daughter, had painted his toenails and braided his hair as he slept yesterday. Tyrell studied Celine under the towel, small capable hands fisting her backpack. He studied those hands—compact and strong, just like her. Unpainted nails, blunt working tips and white knuckles—she was in a snit, all right. So was he. He wasn't happy about discovering his shocking interest in a woman who wanted to destroy him.

He decided to let her sulk and turned to stuff wood into the old iron stove to warm the cabin. She'd tromped into his retreat; he wasn't the offender. He simply wanted to take time to realign his life…without distraction. Tyrell wasn't a man to be distracted easily. He glanced back at her. She sat very still. Too still.

He could almost feel the whack of his mother's behave-yourself wooden spoon on his shoulder. The Blaylock males were trained to honor and treat women well. That spoon now belonged to his sister, Else, and she wouldn't have been happy with him packing this fierce little fireball into his sacred lair.

He scowled at Celine Lomax, troublemaker in his life. He knew he had a savage temper, the surface of which was only scratched even when he discovered Hillary and her father's rejection. He knew that of all the Blaylocks, he was perhaps the most elemental, and that was why he protected himself with an icy veneer. Deep within him, Tyrell knew that he had inherited arrogance and passion from his conquistador and Apache ancestors. He'd learned to conceal it early, and even in lovemaking, he was controlled. But the mountain fed his need to release that savage passion and here, in the wilds, he was free of tethers.

Tyrell studied Celine's damp, gleaming legs. He could almost feel them around him, the slender feminine muscles tightening— His body lurched sensually, unexpectedly. He frowned at the towel covering Celine's head and crossed his arms over his bare chest. She'd invaded his woman-free retreat. Still bitter about Hillary's defection, he wanted a temporary breather from the whole female sex and he did not like bumps in his life. Celine was definitely a strawberry-blond bump.

He swallowed tightly, fear rising in him. Maybe she was crying. Hillary cried prettily to get her way, some new bauble or a glittering social event that he didn't want to attend; Celine's cry would be genuine. His stomach clenched again. Celine Lomax was too real, emotions pouring off her like molten lava. He ran his hand over his stomach as an old ulcer threatened to start up; one delicate sob from Celine and he didn't trust himself. He scowled at her; she was unbalancing not only his life, but his emotions. A man who prided himself on cool logic, Tyrell looked at her uncertainly and waited.

From beneath the towel, she spoke quietly, biting the words. "You're bigger and stronger. It's a typical male ploy to use strength when threatened. But you're outmatched."

Tyrell didn't like the bully-image she'd just hurled at him. He did like those flashing green eyes. Celine Lomax was definitely a passionate woman, all engines running full speed ahead, the air humming around her. Her hair seemed to foam into a brilliant, curling mass around her head, framing her small, set face. He pushed away the grin playing around his mouth. "Oh? How so?"

She ripped the towel away and stood. She jammed on her

glasses and lifted both strawberry-blond eyebrows. "Because I'm right. I'll prove that I'm right," she stated firmly.

Tyrell almost admired her. Her loyalty to the cruel man who had torn apart lives was unquestionable. Cutter Lomax was notorious for his temper and his schemes.

Hillary's loyalties ran to herself and money; this woman had wagered everything on a man's word—a grandfather she loved deeply—without question.

She glanced around his neat cabin, the wood flooring planks he had just repaired, the single bed and spartan table and chairs. "So this is what I've reduced you to. Not quite the old upscale town house, is it? The sunken living room, designer furniture, that neat little office with a big window overlooking the city? Oh, my. I hope you're not missing that pretty stainless-steel kitchen and the fancy gadgets. What? No cappuccino maker?"

Tyrell did miss that cappuccino maker. Now he knew how she'd gotten Mason's top client list. She had mentioned enough names to seem authentic. "Don't tell me. The maid, right?"

"Hey, Elaina was glad for the help that day. She's got a brood at home, you know. The youngest had the flu and was up all night. I helped her clean her house, of course, and she did need the money—her husband is out of work and it was Christmas. I liked her and just helped tidy a bit. I went home with her and she took a luxury bath while I cooked supper and helped the kids with homework."

She scanned the cabin, taking in the paperbacks neatly stacked against the wall and the kerosene lantern on the table next to the rough-hewn, homemade bed. "I'd expect a black-silk-sheet guy like you to hole up in something more classy than a mountain cabin." She hitched up the backpack. "Gee whiz, no high-priced entertainment center, wide-screen TV and sound system here. Got to run. I've got a lot to do, taking Lomax land back."

Tyrell struggled to keep his expression impassive. He really resented that little tic above his left eye.

She glanced around at the cabin again. "You can't face them, can you? Tyrell, the Blaylock failure. Ruined by a Lomax. I'll bet you brought a consolation prize here, some woman all sympathetic and sweet. Most men like someone around to make them feel all big and strong when they're down."

"You're all wet, Lomax, in more ways than one. You'll get sick out there in the cold rain because you've been stubborn. Then you won't be able to dig out those nasty little land-grabbing secrets." Tyrell stared meaningfully at the wet sweater clinging to her chest. For just a heartbeat, he wondered about those freckles on that silky skin and how they would taste. Then he pushed away the idea of Celine's compact body against his, beneath his. He was getting tired of being pitched into an overstuffed bin of "typical males."

"I'm wearing a backpack, Blaylock. I carry spares and a raincoat," she tossed back and glanced around for a separate room in which to change.

When her questioning look returned to him, Tyrell crossed his arms over his bare chest and looked steadily at her. "Take your pick of any room you want," he said and glanced meaningfully around the single room.

When she blushed and averted her face, he knew with disgust that she fascinated him. That he wanted to protect her. That nothing would be right until he drew that sassy mouth beneath his and kissed her.

"Stop glowering, Blaylock. You're starting to steam. I'll step outside to change."

"No. I'll go outside," he said and walked from the cabin, slamming the door after him. He resented that bit of temper, the savage part of him he'd always controlled. As he stood under the porch, watching the sheets of gray rain and brooding over the invasion in his life, Celine opened the door and looked up at him. Dressed in a yellow slicker with a hood, jeans and firemen's boots, she found him in the shadows. A golden red

curl clung, gleaming, to the yellow hood, her glasses like flashing gray steel in the dim light. "Be seeing you. Ta-ta," she
said lightly, then stepped down from the porch and trudged off
into the sodden forest.

Tyrell glared at her and fought the growl rising in his throat.
Surrounded by tall pines and fir and with cougars and bears
hunting prey, she looked like a child merrily skipping off for
the school bus on a rainy day. He wouldn't be waiting at home
with chicken soup when she caught a cold and returned.

He shook his head. If she made it past the creek, she'd be
fine; few people could cross the dangerous creek in torrential
rains. Tyrell ran his hands through his wet hair and they caught
on Cindi's "Braveheart" braids. He tore off his soggy moccasins and his painted toenails mocked him. The fire in the old
stove caused him to feel guilty and he didn't like the nettling
burden; he should stay in his nice warm cabin and forget about
Celine Lomax, and leave her to her hot-tempered fate.

Tyrell again growled low in his throat and knew that his first
take on Celine Lomax was right. She was trouble. Blaylock
males were trained to take care of and respect women. There-
fore— With a decisive gesture, he shot out a hand to turn down
the damper on the stove, slowing the flames. While the fire
lowered, Tyrell tore off his wet jeans and dragged on new ones,
pushed his feet into socks and boots and lashed them tightly.
Celine Lomax would not be on his guilt list, his family was
already occupying it.

*When his father called that last time, Tyrell should have
come home.* He didn't, and then his parents were gone, killed
in an accident on icy roads.

Tyrell reached for a thermos. He would not be responsible
for Celine Lomax, once he got her off his mountain.

"Maybe I was a bit hasty. My temper has a tendency to
cause me to get into trouble at times," Celine muttered as she
clung to a branch, dangling just inches above a swollen, angry

creek. If the branch broke, she'd be swept away. Above her, a huge black bear was watching her struggles. "Shoo," she shouted. "I'm all out of gingersnaps."

She looked up at the man standing on the ground above her. "Oh, hello," she managed cheerfully and tried for a smile. The branch she was clinging to began to crack, resenting her weight.

Within the hood of his yellow slicker, Tyrell Blaylock's dark face scowled down at her. Then his hand shot down to claim her wrist, and in a second, he hauled her up and to her feet. The branch cracked and hurled into the foaming, rushing swollen creek.

"I was doing just fine," Celine said, returning his glare. She was bone-chillingly cold, her muddy jeans plastered against her legs. She struggled against the hand that cupped the back of her head while Tyrell wiped a clean red bandanna over her muddy face. She gasped for air and pushed at him.

He held her more tightly and mopped the cloth over her face one more time. Tyrell Blaylock's slow devastating grin knocked the air she'd just reclaimed from her terror. "Typical. Now this is where you tell me that you were right and I was wrong, right?"

"Are you always this mouthy?" With one finger, he hooked her glasses from her face; he edged aside his raincoat and began cleaning them with the bottom of his black sweatshirt.

She sniffed. "I'm a Lomax, remember. I speak my mind," she stated in a very proper tone. She watched him, warily as his grin remained. She plucked her glasses from him and thrust them on. Her quick mind shot for his problems like a dart on its way to the big red X. "So things aren't that good with your family, either, huh? You can't go to them and ask for money, can you, hotshot?"

The scowl jerked back. Tyrell's jaw tightened and she knew that she'd hit a tender wound. She almost felt sorry for him. He looked like a shaggy outcast, scarred and wary of kindness.

She almost put her hand on his cheek. But she couldn't soothe a Blaylock; her grandfather had cursed her kind heart more than once. Cutter had said they were a treacherous lot, all tall and dark and moody, especially the men. They were hunters, Cutter had said, and savages beneath the fancy manners they used with women.

Because she'd betrayed Cutter's memory, she dug in and attacked. "You had everything you wanted, didn't you? I'll bet your family missed you when you tore off into the world with all those scholarships in your fist. I checked your favorite airline's records…you didn't visit that much and when you did, you didn't stay. Jasmine telephone calls were few since you were eighteen. Oh, you came back for your brothers' weddings, but you didn't stay. So, there's big family trouble, and it's a close family from what I heard at the gas station. So you must have hurt them. It's an easy deduction. You're up here. They're down in the valley."

"We visit," he explained tightly, and glanced across the creek to the bear. "Let's go."

She crossed her arms. She'd let him off the hook for now. Her family life had been yells and threats and pain and revenge. Close, demonstrative and loving families were not in her experience, despite her love for Cutter and her father. She had believed in her grandfather without that comfort.

Tyrell had his soft spots and one of hers was not to be treated like a delicate piece of fluff. She'd managed her own life since she was old enough to feed herself. "I'm not going anywhere with you and do not pick me up again. I'm not a child. That typical macho stuff won't work with me and besides that, you look like you've had enough of a bad day. You should go back to your nice little cabin. Stay there, why don't you, while I tidy up my grandfather's claim."

"Uh-huh." He glanced at the tree that had just been torn free by the rushing, churning water. He fished a small thermos bottle from the rain jacket he was wearing and thrust it at her.

Exhausted, determined to take nothing from a Blaylock, Celine hesitated before her hands settled on the warm thermos bottle.

"It's coffee," said the man who wasn't her prince. His voice was raw, as if something was sticking low in his throat and couldn't decide whether to come out as a growl or a groan. He looked tense and angry. "Warmed over, but hot. Are you going to drink it, or love it?"

She realized she'd been smoothing the shape with one hand, an up and down motion, enjoying the warmth on her frozen fingers. She studied him as she twisted the cup free from the bottle. She poured the hot coffee into the cup and said, "I suppose you're going to catch a cold and blame it on me."

The sound coming from Tyrell was definitely a choked growl.

"You're afraid of me, aren't you?" she pushed, smirking at her triumph. She sipped the hot coffee. "Ah, there's nothing like a slug of hot coffee on a rainy day. But don't think coffee will make points with me. I'm not backing off."

An hour and a half later, she wished she hadn't gone to sleep on Tyrell's hard shoulder. She sniffed delicately, her nose against his throat. Scented of wood smoke and leather and that darkly intense, brooding scent, Tyrell tensed, glaring down at her; he edged slightly away. She pushed herself into the opposite corner. "I'm not happy, Blaylock," she muttered drowsily, trying to push away the heavy weight of lost sleep. "You can't just carry me down a mountain, and shove me into your four-wheeler."

The sleek, roomy, leather-cushioned monster cost more than thirty of her junkyard pickups, bonded by wire and tape, and running on bald tires. "I'll bet you're behind on the payments for this rig."

"Don't talk." Tyrell's big dark hand tightened on the steering wheel, the other shifting the floor gear expertly. The dashboard lights glowed on the taut planes of his face. At that moment, he did look like his conquistador ancestors.

"You can't handle the truth, can you? That your family land was built on the destruction of the rightful owner? Where are we going?" She studied the tall pine trees on the narrow dirt road, lasered by the vehicle's lights.

"I am taking you out of my life." The words were clipped and cold, quivering with frustration.

"You can try, Blaylock," she said, burrowing into the warm blanket he had briskly tucked around her. She yawned and stretched, and tried valiantly to open her eyes.

The next time she awoke Tyrell was carrying her—backpack, blanket and all—up the stairs of a lighted porch. Celine studied his profile, that set jaw, the muscle tensing in his cheek. Too bad his black, glossy lashes were so long and straight, shielding his eyes; she wanted to revel in how she'd shaken his safe little world, to see his fear. A tall, dark woman with a friendly face opened the house's door the same time as Celine tried to squirm out of Tyrell's arms. He held her tightly against him. Too close and too warm. He looked at her in a narrowed, hot, steamy way and his body seemed to ripple around her.

"See? I told you, you'd catch a cold," she crowed and shot him her best smirk. His nostrils seemed to flare, his face tightening and darkening. A nasty little tic in his cheek began; the vein in his temple surged.

Celine blinked. Tyrell Blaylock looked nothing like the suit-clad steel stiletto she'd seen on that New York street corner. She had the strange and fascinating notion that this man was not far from his Native American and Spanish ancestors and that now, he wanted to carry her off to his isolated home. She stared at him and wondered why he held her so close, his body seeming to hum to hers.

Her hand, resting on his chest, picked up the hard staccato beat of his heart; heated vibrations that she did not understand started all over her body.

Tyrell glared at her. There was that slight flare of his nostrils again, a tic over his left eye. "You're an emotional man, Tyrell Blaylock. Maybe too sensitive for your job in New York. I did you a favor."

The woman at the door laughed outright, undaunted by his glare. "Tyrell? Sensitive?"

"Take... *this,* Else. She's muddy and she's got a mouth that never stops. Her name is Celine Lomax. She needs a place to stay for the night," he said to the woman who resembled him. He dropped Celine to her feet, snagged her neck with a big, warm hand and shoved her inside. As though an afterthought, he reached inside to rip his blanket from her. He eyed her darkly with enough impact to lift the hair on her nape, then he closed the door between them.

Fully awake now, Celine blinked. A cat was twining around her legs, a friendly-looking man was smiling at her from the living room, and the house was definitely a home, fresh with scents of children and baking bread. Over her dress, Else wore an apron and a small sleepy child tucked on her hip. This was a Blaylock home and one Celine might tear apart.

She wasn't certain what to say, or how to act. Delicious aromas wafted to her, and as a reminder that she hadn't eaten, her stomach clenched. Latticed pies sat on a counter, and next to the smiling man was a rocking chair still teetering as if Else had been rocking the child.

Homes terrified Celine—she knew little of them. The warmth in this home reached out to her like a magnet; she'd dreamed of homes like this, and a mother—terror rose, chilling her. She had to escape. "He's getting away," she explained hurriedly and opened the door.

Else laughed aloud. "I know. You're welcome to stay here tonight. But if you're going to catch my brother, you'd better hurry. My brothers get moldy when they're not stirred up and Tyrell is definitely— You've got him on the run. I wouldn't lose any advantage by letting him get away like that."

"I do? You wouldn't?" Celine turned to study Tyrell's quick stride toward his four-wheeler. "I do have him on the run, don't I?"

"He had the last say, you know. I wouldn't let him get away with that if I were you."

"You wouldn't?"

Else grinned, cuddling the sleepy child closer. "If I were you and he dumped me like a stray cat, I'd want him to pay."

"Thanks. You're right. I can't let him get away with shoving me around." Celine took a second to study Else, the matron of the Blaylock family. The gas station attendant had said that Else had ruled her brothers and had taken over her mother's place in the community. Celine shivered; she didn't know what a mother's place was—her mother had walked out.

Else hugged the sleeping child tighter to her and nodded, her eyes dancing with amusement. Celine pushed away that little quiver of warmth, a woman who for the moment agreed with her, almost like a friend. Celine hurried out the door; she couldn't think about Else Blaylock Murphy now. She had to get Tyrell.

Tyrell Blaylock presented a good, solid target. Above those long jeaned legs and narrow hips, his black sweatshirt covered a good rangy width of back and shoulders. Celine hurled the weight of her body at him; she hit him squarely in the back with both open hands. He lurched forward a step and pivoted in one motion, crouching slightly. "I've had enough of you for one day, Lomax," he said between his teeth as he straightened. He flung the blanket he'd been carrying onto his four-wheeler.

"You deserve it. You had no right to drop me off like an unwanted cat. What's the matter? Can't take a Lomax? Afraid of me?" she shot at him. As a child, before she'd learned to fend for herself, she'd been shoved into other places and some of them weren't friendly. She knew she'd been unwanted by her mother, but she didn't have to take that as an adult—from a Blaylock. Unknowingly Tyrell had really hit a sore spot.

"You're pushing, Lomax," he said between his teeth. "I don't like it."

"Really?" She slathered the word in delight; she'd gotten to him. She launched her best smirk at him.

His eyes narrowed as he towered over her. Battling her instincts to step back, Celine deepened her smirk up at him. She knew she was getting to him because that tiny muscle above his left eye started quivering.

"It's the dimple," he muttered with disgust, just before he pulled her into his arms and fused his mouth to hers.

She'd been kissed before—when she was an experimenting teenager. She hadn't had time to explore her own needs, and that one brief painful teenage experience with sex was enough to last forever.

Stunned, she stared at Tyrell's closed lashes, the line between his brows. Enclosed by his arms, by the heat coming from his body, Celine reached for his hair to pull him away. Her fists latched to the sleek damp strands and then the incredible heat and hunger of his mouth upon hers caused her mind to blank for a heartbeat.

He's devouring me, burning me, she thought distantly as her fingers curled into the strands and her eyes closed to seal in the pleasure riding her. Tyrell's open hands claimed her close, one riding low on her hips, the other at the back of her head, supporting her and pressing her close to his body.

His obviously aroused body.

She wanted to stop and think, to dissect her options, but the tropical storm flashing inside her burned out any logic. She simply felt. Tasted. Hungered and dived into all the exciting textures surrounding her. Tyrell slanted his mouth, taking the kiss deeper, his hand surged beneath her bottom and lifted her firmly up to him.

She burned, his ragged breath sweeping across her face. She couldn't let the excitement escape her, and locked her arms around his shoulders. Tyrell groaned, trembled and hefted her higher. Locking her legs around his hips, wrestling to keep that heat and excitement close, Celine almost sent them toppling to the ground. Tyrell spun and leaned back against his four-wheeler, his tongue flicked greedily at her lips, his face burning against hers. His big hands cupped her bottom, and when his mouth tore away from hers, she cried out softly.

His black stare shot down to lock on her shirt, her breasts pushed against his chest. He began to tremble and because she couldn't resist his uncertain, wary look, she stroked his hot cheek. He looked as if he'd explode, his familiar scowl down at her deepening. "Now you've done it," he muttered and placed his hands on her waist, firmly removing her.

She ached for that warmth, for the hard safety of his arms. She didn't know what to do, her body trembling.

Tyrell impatiently mopped the curls from her face, studied her and shook his head. He looked up at the cloudy night and groaned. He stared at Else, who was standing in front of the open door, her arms crossed in a forbidding stance. He issued a bearlike, frustrated growl, ran his hands through his hair and down his jaw and glared at Celine. She hovered there, stunned, licking her sensitive bottom lip and tasting his hunger.

Celine couldn't worry about the matron of the Blaylocks defending her little brother. The Precious Baby of the Blaylocks had— Stunned, Celine touched her bottom lip. It throbbed and tasted of him, dark and moody and exciting. "You bit me," she said. *"You...bit...me,"* she repeated, her tone rising indignantly as she wondered where to hit him. "That was a definite nip. Just exactly why would you kiss or nip me?"

Glaring at her, he didn't answer and he had to pay. To add just one more torment in Tyrell Blaylock's life, she turned to Else and yelled cheerfully, "I'm not pregnant."

The shocking insinuation that she could be expecting Tyrell's baby was certain to cost him.

Tyrell did that frustrated bear-growl thing again, low in his throat, and grabbed her shoulders; he turned and pushed her toward the house. She dug in her heels and turned to him. "You're just so typical male, you know. If you can't get something one way, you try for another. Nipping will not be tolerated, Blaylock."

With a dark, threatening look at her, Tyrell jerked open the car door and slid inside. Still staring at her, he flipped on the ignition, jerked the car into gear and tore into the dark, sweet rain-scented night.

Celine stared at him; little aftershocks zipped through her body as though she'd just stepped out of a tropical storm into the cool night. Low in her body was the most peculiar ache. She glanced at Else and found a thumbs-up sign. Celine tried a smirk and it died; she was instantly aware of the cold without Tyrell's arms around her.

At her side, Else placed an arm on Celine's shoulder, ignoring her stiff body. "Well, I guess you gave him something to think about. My brother has been holing up on his mountaintop for six months, rebuilding that run-down old cabin, and you got him down among the living."

Celine snorted. "He's mourning Hillary-poo."

"That out-for-money, moral-less witch," Else stated vehemently and handed Celine a thick turkey-and-cheese sandwich on a paper plate.

Celine's empty stomach clenched at the sight of food. She wanted to reject it, not wanting to take something from a Blaylock, but instead she picked it up and began munching. "Thanks."

"Anytime. Do you want to come inside and have a glass of fresh cow's milk to go with that?"

Celine shook her head, her mouth too stuffed to talk. She studied the older woman, a tall, older and feminine version of Tyrell. She seemed kind and a friend. "I'd like you to stay with us. Just for the night," Else said.

"My tent is in my pickup. It's just up the road. Thank you,

but I'd better be going,'' Celine said and hitched her backpack up on her shoulder. She didn't want to think about the Blaylocks being kind and friendly. There was no reason for the Blaylocks to accept her, to make a stranger welcome. Cutter had said they weren't to be trusted and the unexpected warmth raised her guard.

Then there was that Tyrell-kiss. She wanted to yank it from her and stomp it dead with her boots. She wanted to kill the taste of his hunger and the racing excitement within her. She wanted to relieve her temper with a really good yell.

She was just around the bend of the tree-lined country road, when the sound of an engine purred behind her. A glance at the vehicle without headlights told her it was Tyrell's. She kept on walking, turning to punctuate her dislike of him with a glare. He didn't take the hint, parking beside the road while she set up her tiny tent beside her pickup. Then his headlamps seared her and Tyrell drove away.

Celine threw a rock in his direction and knew it wouldn't hit the gleaming metal monster. ''Take that, Blaylock,'' she muttered. Thanks to Tyrell Blaylock, the man she'd ruined, it was going to be a long, angry night.

Three

Tyrell slapped the file on Roman Blaylock's desk. His brother's upscale computer had provided everything Tyrell needed to dig into Celine's life. The printed pages left little to the imagination; Celine had had a hard life. Her resources were next to nothing and after the deaths of her father and grandfather, she'd worked overtime—taking overseas and any high-paying job—to build a small nest egg. Those funds from an international bank had been withdrawn just days before her arrival on his mountain. Celine had pitted everything against the Blaylocks and on Cutter's lie. "Thanks for the use of the computer."

An older brother, just as tall and powerful, Roman stared at him levelly, reflecting the same strong planes and dark Blaylock features. "I'm glad you stopped by. Make it a point, will you? But not at bedtime?"

Tyrell's family didn't know of the cracks in his life, but they knew that he'd come back to roam the wild mountains he loved above the valley. They knew he needed peace and didn't question his life away from them.

Roman's ranch held part of the original Blaylock land that Cutter Lomax had claimed was stolen from him. Roman was also the executor of Boone Llewlyn's estate, which included his ranch and ten thousand acres—minus one thousand that had been signed over to Paloma Blaylock, Rio's wife. Roman, his wife, Kallista, his son, Kipp, and Cindi, his adopted daughter, lived in the addition; Roman had an up-to-date office in Boone's turn-of-the-century house.

"It's eleven o'clock at night, my son Kipp is dreaming one-year-old toddler dreams, and my wife is waiting for me," Roman stated, in a firm get-lost tone. "I'd appreciate it if for tonight you'd find someone else to bother, or hike on back up to that cabin. You've been at my house twice in three days. Gee, why am I so lucky? You've wintered up there in Micah's old cabin since you came back in January. Then suddenly, you come down to suck up my wife's lasagna and sprawl, stuffed full, on my couch. Now you need a computer after months without one."

Tyrell lifted an eyebrow. He'd felt like a stray cat on Roman's doorstep. The warmth of his brother's household and his obvious deep love for his wife caused Tyrell to feel even more of an outsider. He'd missed so much.

He'd resented the need for cooking other than his own, but he wanted to see his new nephew, to hold him. Tyrell needed to see Roman's adopted daughter, Cindi, who was lively and a real challenge. He needed to know that simple loving lives went on in his family. "You probably gave Cindi the idea to paint my toenails and braid my hair."

He should have been there for his parents, all those missing years. Instead he'd shot out into the world like a bolt, cutting his way to the top, clustering numbers around him like friends. That life had been hollow and cold, he saw that now. He'd missed so much. He was an outsider now, the lone wolf of the pack.

He'd also been an outsider to the social side of his financial world. Yet he'd stayed. If Celine hadn't interfered, he would have been deep in power plays and building profit. Eventually he would have seen the emptiness of his life and needed more, but she hurried the process.

Roman's knuckle-rap on Tyrell's head was familiar and just as annoying as it was years ago. "Before you figured out that boys didn't like girl stuff, Else used to dress you up with her dolls. Mmm. I have a picture of that somewhere. The Blaylock brothers, our sister and you at three, wearing a dress— Ouch! No elbows in ribs.... Celine Lomax. You came down from your cave for her."

"To get rid of her," Tyrell corrected darkly. "You're going to hold that picture over me until we're both too old to tangle, aren't you?" He sank into the desk chair to glower at Roman. He'd forgotten how close his family was, and damned himself for forgetting. He didn't want to look at the pictures, to look at his parents alive and happy and their brood around him. It hurt too much. He'd shot out of the Blaylock nest as soon as he could and he'd always been too busy to return for more than a few days. *He should have come back; he should have stayed. Instead he'd traded his family for a demanding, profitable career.* "Else must have called you."

"She worries, and you've never tried to dump a spitting-mad woman on her doorstep before. She said you were really worked up, and it was the first time that all the Blaylock boys— she's going to call us 'boys' forever, you know—were all stirred up at once.... She said she doesn't have to worry about you going moldy up in that cabin with Celine around.... Lomax," Roman frowned, testing the name. "Any relation to Cutter?"

Tyrell nodded. He decided not to tell Roman about Celine's quest; she'd be gone soon enough.

Roman shook his head and stood. "She's got plenty of nerve, coming back to country where her grandfather tried every crime possible. Cutter was notorious. He hurt a lot of people and it's said that he murdered, too. I believe that, from the scar I saw on Grandpa Luke. Cutter didn't want the sheriff, our grandfather, taking him in, or stopping him from abusing that horse. But Cutter was in jail more than he was out, until the judge sent him to the penitentiary for land fraud. Grandma was the only woman Cutter ever treated with respect. Lomax was a hot-tempered, red-haired and freckled-faced thug."

"Celine doesn't know that. She loved him." Celine's loyalty was unquestionable; Hillary's had shredded at the first test. Tyrell wondered how he could have come so close to marrying her.

Roman frowned. "She'll find out soon enough. People won't say much at first, because her name is Lomax. If they get to know and like her, they may. Too many people know and equate the Lomax name with hard times and pain."

"I know." Celine had inherited the famed Lomax temper, red hair and freckles. And on her, it wasn't bitter and mean, but bewitching and very feminine. He rubbed his hand over his jeaned leg. Tyrell wished he could remove the silky feel of her curls twining around his fingers, and the taste of her mouth. Or those sultry green eyes, drowsy with his kiss.

Something light and easy and happy danced inside him when he looked at her. He wasn't certain he liked the unstable emotion; as an adult he'd always seen profit and loss and serious situations. He slapped his hand flat on the Celine Lomax file. That unfamiliar feeling would align soon, as soon as he dissected it—or tore Celine from Jasmine and the valley.

Nothing was going to happen to his family's lands and nothing would happen to her.

He did know that Celine Lomax had jarred his basic savage needs to claim—to possess a woman. Tyrell wiped his hand across his tense jaw, uncomfortable with the jolting need he hadn't suspected in his well-manufactured life. All the fire and passion he'd shoved into a drawer years ago came tearing out when he'd reached for her. He'd chosen Hillary to be his corporate partner, more than his wife. Bred to corporate life and society, she would have complemented his business talent.

He ran his thumb across his lips, remembering the silky texture of Celine's. *Celine's soft mouth tasted like roses and fire at the same time.* And she was an innocent. He'd been away from innocence too long. He could easily hurt her. When she discovered Cutter's lies, she'd have enough pain to last forever. And shame. Tyrell knew how it felt to visualize and work for what you thought was best and then have it shatter into dust. Out of habit, he tapped the keys on Roman's electric adding machine. Automatically Tyrell picked up a balance sheet, ran a finger down it. He added the numbers with flying fingers, and noted, "You've got a problem here. As Boone's executor, you should know that Boone's orchid house is costing plenty without a profit."

This was what Tyrell knew—numbers, profit, loss, investments. They were safe; his emotions weren't, not with Celine's wide-open passionate, and yet untutored, kiss lurking in him.

"Boone wanted orchids, not profit. And Jasmine could use an investment-numbers whiz like you. Think about it. I want to spend more time with my wife and son. You could handle some of Boone's accounts." Roman rose and placed his hand on Tyrell's shoulder. With his other hand, he picked up the file and slapped it in Tyrell's hand. "I'm glad you're back, little brother. It's been a long time and we missed you. I'm glad you got what you wanted from the computer information banks. Now, out. Or you can sleep upstairs in one of Boone's bedrooms. I do not want you in the addition where Kallista and I sleep, until morning."

"I've been back," Tyrell said in his defense. He wondered how he'd ever make up the nineteen years he'd spent away.

He noted that Roman was the same—steadfast and unquestioning when his brothers needed something.

"Sure. Back for weddings and funerals and off again. And always with a faraway look in your eye, as if you were thinking of leaving before you really settled in. You practically grew a telephone in your ear while you were here. Boone did that same thing, you know. Left here for years and came back to his roots. I hope you find what you need, little brother. It's pretty tame here in Jasmine. Not a corporation ripe for takeover in sight."

"I hope it stays that way. The same. Good and solid. Roman, I regret leaving, missing that time with Mom and Dad. And all of you."

"You'll work it out," said Roman, a quiet man who said exactly what he believed. "You came back here to think and that's good. Everyone needs to stop and do that in their lives, to find their true path. It's not hard to step back into our family. I know. Kallista dragged me back into the family when I felt apart."

Hours later, Tyrell gave up sleeping in Boone's old bed. He made the bed neatly and passed silently from the house, carrying Celine's file.

In the predawn light, he moved swiftly up the mountain, wanting to be alone, to kill his need to see Celine Lomax again. To taste her. To dive into the wild storm of textures and colors and heat that one kiss had bred.

He'd wanted to tear away their clothes and have that full, rich woman's body then, careless of everything else. That need had shaken him; he'd never needed anyone, and now he did. The new experience gave him insight into his brothers' expressions when they looked at their wives. He was outside all that, the family he'd left behind. Tyrell picked up his pace, pushing the sensual need away from him, gathering back his control. He wanted logic and plenty of it, not the taste of her inexperienced lips on his, like silky hungry butterflies playing timidly against him.

In his cabin, Tyrell flipped open the file, studying it. Celine Lomax had had a hard life, and from the look of her battered pickup, she'd spent everything to prove her grandfather right. There would be no reclaiming Cutter's honor; he'd lashed it to pieces while he was alive. Celine had put herself through the surveyor's course, she'd paid her father's and grandfather's medical bills and for their simple burials. Her grades weren't tops, but with two jobs and ill family to care for, she'd placed solidly in her class. She was valued by her company and took the highest paying jobs, which were usually the hardest. She'd worked all over the world and she should have better—she'd stripped her finances bare just days before arriving. Tyrell's hand slapped the file closed. He could just imagine the life she'd led, growing up in the same house with Cutter Lomax and his son's dark moods. Tyrell had put out queries about her mother and it was only a matter of time before something turned up.

Tyrell had tasted innocence on her lips—an erotic taste, too sweet to believe, tugging violently at needs he didn't want to explore. He ran his hand across his bare chest and remembered the sway of her hips in his headlights. The slight quiver as she tromped along, glaring back at him, was enticing.

Tyrell groaned and rubbed his hands over his face. He had no reason to be concerned about Celine Lomax. But she'd better leave him alone.

In the next two days, Celine discovered that Jasmine didn't have a thrift or secondhand shop. There wasn't a need; everyone pitched in for a needy family. Secondly, the extensive Blaylock family was everywhere. Dan's wife, Hannah, was a decorator. Else and Joe Murphy had their own brood and were now grandparents. Logan and his wife had five children; Roman's wife Kallista owned the Bisque Café, a do-it-yourself ceramic shop. Rio's wife Paloma owned half of Jasmine's feed store and had developed a museum of country life in Jasmine.

There were aunts and uncles in a Western Camelot setting. Boone's white two-story turn-of-the-century home stood atop a knoll overlooking Jasmine and the valley.

Everyone had loved Boone Llewlyn, especially children. Cutter had made him sound money-grasping and arrogant. At the mention of her last name, the clerk at the grocery store had frowned and tensed. The woman had been guarded and her friendly smile had died.

If Celine hadn't been so hungry, she wouldn't have eaten all the food Else had brought to her. The kindness sharpened Celine's distrust of the Blaylocks: she doubted that Else had cooked too much to feed her family, or that she just happened to have it in the car when she dropped by Celine's tent.

Celine took one day to drive around the countryside, praying her pickup's tires could last on the unpaved farm roads. Cutter had been right. His poor circumstances, and his family's would not have occurred if he had been able to keep the Lomax property. The land was rich and flourishing. He could have been one of the elderly men sitting on the spit and whittle bench in the small city park. But he wasn't. And Celine's father, Link Lomas, died a bitter man. They'd swallowed their dreams with whiskey.

Cutter had loved Garnet Marie Holmes Blaylock; he'd said that Luke Blaylock had wooed her away with lies.

Celine inhaled, checked her locked pickup, which held her tent and few belongings. She scanned the child's red wagon behind her. It held everything she needed for basic surveying on the mountain. The metal detector was secondhand and she'd spent hours cleaning the transit—a device to line up surveyor markers. "Betty," the transit, was a pawnshop find and worn, but good; the telescope was in good shape, just a scratch or two, complete with the plumb bob that hung beneath it to establish the true vertical. The carefully packed, sensitive tripod had lost its smooth finish years ago, and its second layer of bright yellow was chipped, but all three legs were sturdy, supporting the heavy transit.

Two other tripods and a "surveyor's stick," a rod with a prism that focused with the transit's laser beam, would allow her to do the work by herself. She could work from a "back site point" to a "control point," and focus on the "foresight" point. By running back and forth between the three sites—no easy job for one person—she could manage. Loaded with topographical maps of the area, she would drive heavy nails into the ground to align with her plumb bob as a "control point." A small, but effective chain saw would help to clear concealing brush. Celine believed she could do the work alone. *If the chiseled description from one marking stone had been tampered with, sandblasted to erase the legal description of sections and directions, she would know it.*

Computerized surveys would give her what had been fed into them, incorrect information from the Blaylock deeds. She wanted to use Cutter's memories: a bent tree, a pile of rocks and paces from objects; she'd use old abstracts, homesteading journals, diaries and the local papers. This first quick trip she only intended preliminary research; the Blaylock lies would be hard to untangle. First, basic research, then more in depth. The surveyor in a neighboring town wasn't talking; he didn't like another professional in his territory, especially a woman. "Okay, so I shouldn't have told him off and put my muddy boot on his desk," Celine muttered. "Maybe that was a bad start."

Small enough to travel on narrow paths, her child's wagon had been reinforced, a shoulder harness added and tall sturdy tricycle tires added. If need be, she could lash it to her back. But for the most part, it pulled along behind her just fine.

Celine studied the jutting forbidding cliffs and the spot where Boone Llewlyn's cabin would be located, near the gold mine Cutter claimed was rightfully his. She scanned a distance away to another place, where unseen, Tyrell's cabin snuggled amid the pine forest.

Tyrell Blaylock. Just the name caused her temper to roll, her body to tense. He'd kissed her as if he'd found everything he wanted in a woman, with a hunger that shattered and invited, soothed and hurt and terrified. Locked together in that kiss, Celine had pitted herself against him—diving into all that lurked, exciting her, all those textures and scents— "Okay. He unnerved me. I reacted as if I were still in the field, the best pole climber in the survey crew. Now that is just disgusting."

She had had the most incredible sensation that Tyrell wanted to carry her off and make her his, to possess her, to make love to her. At the time, he'd trembled, heated against her.

Celine's breath caught, pounded from her by her own thunderbolts. *Make love to her.* With Tyrell's body close up against her it was obvious he desired her. She knew the mechanics of an aroused male—she'd heard her father and grandfather guffawing about their conquests enough. "Some women like it rough," Cutter had said. "Making love" hadn't applied to her only teenage experience in the back seat of a car.

"Just typical," she muttered, fitting the harness to her shoulders and trying to push away the sweetness of the kiss, a mystical hunger that enticed.

Celine's eyes narrowed on the mountain forest area where Tyrell's cabin nestled. He had seemed too desperate, maybe he was; on the other hand, maybe his eyesight lacked focus. Desire wasn't usual in the men that passed through Celine's life…mostly her working life, and that was all she'd done since she could remember. "Settle everything with a Casanova act. Tomcat."

She scowled at the quail bursting from the sagebrush as she passed. Tyrell hadn't played a smooth lover—he'd taken, all engines running full open speed. Those big hands had cupped her bottom almost desperately, his mouth burning into hers. There was no tenderness in Tyrell Blaylock in that moment;

he was raw, hungry, devastating, his shields down. And she hadn't been frightened; she'd been in the storm with him, greedily pushing her hands through his hair and holding him close.

Celine wiped the back of her hand across her mouth, trying to push away Tyrell's burning, hungry kiss. "Okay, so he's lonely. Okay, so I haven't kissed that much, maybe it's a man-thing to grab a woman and suck her mouth. *He nipped me!* He actually nipped my lip with his teeth. If he wants a fight, I can give it to him, but I'd never sink to biting. I'm here to get Cutter's land back, and his honor. Cutter said not to trust a Blaylock, and I won't."

Once she performed the preliminary survey, got her ideas aligned, she intended to ruin Tyrell with a survey that would prove Cutter right.

"She looks like a stubborn child in a snit, dragging her wagon behind her," Tyrell muttered as he spotted Celine trudging up the path to Boone Llewlyn's mountain cabin. He shoved the hand plane down the rough-hewn board one more time, needing the strenuous physical exercise since he had met Celine two days ago. A stack of smooth boards, new flooring for an addition to the cabin, mocked him. There should be no reason why his instincts told him to protect Celine Lomax; she'd come to harm him and his family.

She believed Cutter; she'd be hurt to find out his lies and his shady reputation.

Tyrell wiped the sweat from his face with the back of his forearm. Celine would want his portion of the old Blaylock homestead more than the rest. She'd stalked him in New York...and he wanted to track her down now and enjoy those green eyes, one with a brown spot that deepened after their kiss. He snorted. Celine Blaylock did not know how to kiss; she'd been stunned.

She'd been stunned? A man who had always been controlled

even in his hormonal teenage years, he'd been devastated by his reaction to her taste, her scent and those soft little gasps coming from her. Tyrell frowned and rammed the hand plane down the board. He scanned his property—rough woodsy mountains and alpine meadows, none of it fit for large scale ranching. His brothers wanted to ranch and their portions of the old Blaylock homestead sprawled across the valley. But he'd wanted this place, where Micah Blaylock had wintered, where the animals grew thick winter fur, and the water was pure. Untamed and protected by its isolation, his property could support a cow or two, and the air was sweet, scented now of the newly planed wood. He ripped the plane down the board again and tried to push Celine from his mind.

The next morning, he sat by her bedroll, one arm braced across his raised knee; he waited for her to awake. She snuggled down in the sleeping bag like a child without a care— Tyrell scanned the woods, layered with mist and heavy with danger. He studied the woman he wanted off his mountain and out of his mind. Asleep, Celine Lomax was soft and delicate, wisps of her red-gold hair caressing her cheek. One curl fluttered with each breath she took. Her hands, upturned by her face, were small, callused and competent.

He traced a fingertip, delicate and feminine against his own dark one. Tyrell swallowed roughly, remembering the firm, and yet light, touch of her hand at his nape.

That one light touch, just a brush of her hand, had soothed him and yet made him want more. Whatever life Celine had led, she knew how to comfort and she was extremely feminine and soft, despite her tomboy exterior.

Unable to leash himself, he ran a fingertip down her smooth, warm cheek. The tiny freckles delighted him. That pulse at her throat was slow and soft— Tyrell breathed uneasily, quietly. He'd never studied a sleeping woman before, fascinated by each breath, that curl fluttering on her cheek and the one resting against the pulse in her throat; he'd never had the urge to slide in beside a woman and playfully awaken her with kisses.

Tyrell scowled at the woman sleeping peacefully in her sleeping bag. Celine Lomax's effect on him mocked his sensual past, and made his few sexual contacts seem lukewarm. He was a meticulous man, not a bed-hopper. His sexual alliance with Hillary had never been jolting, but he hadn't expected that from her.

The woman who had jolted him for the first time in his life, making him question his other relationships, sighed. Her body arched in sleep, then her lashes jerked open. He caught her hand, just as she reached for a nearby tiny can of pepper spray—bear repellent.

Tyrell smiled tightly, his body tensed, his fingers wrapped around her wrist. "You're trespassing."

He looked at her, all warm and soft from sleep, her silky curls gleaming, and those green eyes, still drowsy, wary and spearing him. The excitement he felt when Celine was awake rushed through him and he fought grinning.

She edged away from his hand. "Don't you dare touch my hair."

"You've got a twig in your hair," he lied, using the excuse to smooth one warm, tempting curl with his fingertip. It twined around his fingertip, snaring him, and within Tyrell something gentle and exquisite quivered.

She eyed him and sat up in her bedroll, fully dressed in a flannel shirt, worn jeans and socks.

Tyrell fought the quiver running through him. He wanted to tug her into his arms and cuddle her. He wanted to protect her. "You could get hurt if you continue with this, Lomax."

Those strawberry-blond eyebrows rose, her jaw hardening. "Threats? You're threatening me?"

He wanted to cradle her warm cheek in his palm, to draw her cheek close to his and to rock her, taking away the pain

she must have had as Cutter's granddaughter. Instead he stood
to look down at her.

She looked the long way up his legs and quickly scrambled
out of her bedroll to stand. Tyrell tried not to smile as she
struggled for every inch of her height, glaring up at him.

"I'm bigger than you, Lomax. And I'm stronger. It's a natural thing—you know, men and women have differences. Get
used to it. So what's on the agenda today?" he asked, the light,
almost eager tone surprising him as much as his anticipation
of seeing how she would react to him. Tyrell sucked in the
cold crisp mountain air; he hadn't realized he liked to tease.

She studied him warily as she sat on her rumpled bedroll
and Tyrell's body lurched into hardness. She jerked on her
boots and began tying them. "You may be bigger and stronger,
but I can handle you."

Tyrell crouched and took the task from her hands, and wondered why. He jerked the leather laces into a bow and returned
her wary look. "What if I'd like another kiss?" he asked, and
knew that he was not a man to tease, but he was with her. Then
he bent his head and took the kiss he craved.

"Get off me," Celine whispered a moment later, her eyes
wide and stunned. "You're mashing me."

"You kissed me back, Lomax," he whispered against her
lips. "You dragged me over you. I was helpless."

"What is it with you, Blaylock?" she asked, in a bewildered
tone. "Have you gone unbalanced, living out here alone without Hillary-poo?"

"This has nothing to do with Hillary." Every instinct told
him that this was the woman with whom he would make love—
someday. He flexed his lower body against hers once and
groaned. He placed his face against her throat where she was
soft and warm and scented of woman, and knew her scent
would haunt him in the midnight hours. Then he forced himself
to roll away from her, coming to stand in one smooth motion.
He closed his eyes against the image of Celine, lying on the

ground, rumpled, warm and softly dazed, and then he turned and walked away.

"Are you going to spy on me all day, Blaylock?" she called after him. "What's the matter? Are you afraid I'll find you or your family moved Cutter's boundary rocks, the markers?"

He stopped, forced himself not to return to her, and continued walking. He hoped she didn't see his hand rub his jaw, a gesture of frustration that reflected the condition of his entire body.

She knew that Tyrell Blaylock tracked her movements as she worked, hunting boundary markers of piled rocks that had been covered by fallen trees and brush. Her shoulders ached from carrying the metal detector used to find the buried metal surveyors' bars.

He'd seen her fall on her bottom and he'd reached to fish her out from a cave that could have held all the answers to the Blaylock's dark deeds. Being dragged out by her booted ankles hadn't made her happy.

Tyrell wore his moccasins, his shirt had opened to reveal his chest, his hair swept away from his harsh features by the scented mountain breeze. He had only laughed at the swing she took at him. That dark, rich laughter had surprised her. She'd stared up at him, her mind blank, before she knew she'd better get her body away. Tyrell Blaylock's black eyes still held laughter when he suddenly became too quiet, just looking at her as if she fascinated him.

"Hello, Lomax," he had said quietly in a sultry tone she didn't understand, but that sent electricity around her body. She didn't understand the intense hot look he shot at her flannel shirt, which had lost an essential button over her bra. He had groaned again, for reasons she did not understand, before he turned and walked away.

"Fine. Run away. I like that, a Blaylock running from a Lomax." She had smirked after him, then shivered as she picked up the metal detector and began sweeping it over the ground. If ever she'd seen a disgusted man, it was Tyrell Blaylock.

The first buried metal boundary marker was where it should have been, and the next. The tree Cutter had described as "fifty or so feet northwest of the three black boulders" was gone.

As she hiked over the portion of the sunlit mountain that now belonged to Tyrell Blaylock, she saw why Cutter had wanted this land. Layered with forests, and small lush alpine meadows, this portion of the Blaylocks' land was untamed, deer grazing with fawns. In the distance a bear sunned on a huge flat boulder. Higher up on the mountains, amid the jutting black and searing red cliffs, mountain sheep leaped from the rocky ledges.

Celine inhaled the fresh, crisp air, scented of pines. She preferred working outside, rather than in an office. Maybe it was because she'd tried to become the grandson Cutter desired. Maybe it was because everything was so clean, without the interoffice power plays that Tyrell would know well.

A few remains of a sweeping fire that almost devoured the rugged mountain pine forests could be seen in a tiny canyon. Cutter had said the Blaylocks pointed a guilty finger at him, that Luke Blaylock had falsely blamed him to get Garnet Marie. What kind of woman would bring a tender look to Cutter's hard eyes?

Why did Tyrell Blaylock's dark, tense looks rivet her boots to the ground and start a heated earthquake within her?

That night when Celine set up camp, she hadn't found the boulder Cutter had said marked his claim. A boulder the size of a "two-car garage" couldn't be moved without heavy machinery; in this rough mountain timberland, equipment that size would have needed a road. There was no road, even overgrown, but she'd found the boundary stone with a chiseled land description marking Blaylock's land.

She ached from dragging the well-packed transit and the

tripods, the wagon loaded with camping supplies and her precious maps. The metal detector's strap had worn a painful strip on her shoulder. The preliminary survey to get her bearings wasn't going well; Cutter's memories of land and trees and stone hadn't appeared. And the big house he'd described as his before the Blaylocks ruined him wasn't in the canyon.

She rubbed her shoulder and then the growing ache across her forehead. Cutter hadn't been back for years, maybe he'd been confused by time and the distances and types of trees distorted. Maybe… Maybe…

The hair on the back of her head stood up and she knew Tyrell Blaylock was near. He stood as if he'd never move, blending in the evening shadows, watching her. "Afraid I'll find something illegal, Blaylock? Waiting to move a few piled rocks in your favor?" she taunted as he walked slowly into her firelight.

She tensed. Dressed much the same as she, a flannel shirt, jeans and a jacket, Tyrell had strapped a sleeping bag to his back. He'd moved like that on the city street—controlled, poised, purposeful. But now his stride wasn't eating up long distances of concrete sidewalk, it was closing the distance between them. Tyrell's mountain man ancestor must have moved the same way, long and lean, striding freely, stalking his prey. Celine shivered, but refused to budge, her fists pushed into her waist. "No biting," she ordered darkly, eyeing him.

"I regret the lapse," he returned just as darkly. He slung the rolled sleeping bag to the ground and hefted a branch at his side; four huge cleaned trout dangled from it. Without a word, Tyrell placed each trout on a stick over the fire to cook. While their fat dropped to sizzle into the fire, he glared at her, his features in the firelight as savage as his ancestors and as forbidding and arrogant. Then he rose to go to the creek, crouching to wash his hands. He stood and scanned the night draping the mountain and whatever trembled inside Celine when she saw Tyrell leaped into life.

He returned to the campfire and Celine flipped him a hard get-lost look. Tyrell smiled coolly and reached to open his sleeping bag.

The action was firm, Tyrell's gaze never leaving her face; he was staying the night. "You're not sleeping here, Blaylock. Not with me."

He sat on a log, stretched his long jeaned legs in front of him, and expertly turned the fish over the fire. She sat on her sleeping bag and tapped her fingers on her thigh. "Why are you here?"

"You're irritating me, Lomax. If you don't have sense enough to camp somewhere safe, someone *with* sense has to stay with you."

"I camp all the time. By myself. Anywhere I want."

"You're not by yourself tonight, Lomax-honey. You're with me." His eyes flickered down her taut body and he smiled slowly, richly, as if he had everything he wanted. "Honey, it's our first date," he drawled smoothly.

"We're not on a date, Blaylock. You're invading my privacy. I was here first. *We are not on a date,*" she repeated hotly.

"You're so easy, Lomax. I like watching you get all hot and bothered." He flipped her towel over her lap, placed one of her plastic plates on it and handed her a fish. "Those potatoes you buried in the coals would taste good with that."

"You were spying on me or you wouldn't know what I'm cooking."

"I was fishing down by the creek. It was hard to miss your yowl. I watched just long enough to see that you weren't badly burned." His grin widened as she scowled at him. He bent to push away the coals from the two big baked potatoes—one she'd planned for tonight and the other to eat cold for tomorrow's lunch. He tossed one foil-wrapped potato by her boots and placed the other on a flat rock. "I'd say you're at a steady simmer right now. But could you save your tirade until after we've had dinner?''

"You're enjoying this, aren't you?" She crunched her elbows into her stomach to stop the hungry growling noises. She flopped the trout onto a flat rock, placed a section onto her plastic plate and wished she could resist. She picked away the foil and added the potato, fishing out her carton of butter—she wasn't sharing that with him.

"Eat. You'll feel better," Tyrell said in a tone that held more humor than sympathy.

"So this is what dropouts do? Run around mountainsides looking for people who do not want to be disturbed?" she taunted around the tasty bite of fish. "Or is it really dropping out? Maybe it's because you do not have any money or anywhere else to run to, eh? I'd be careful about selling this land because it's not really yours. It's Lomax land.''

He ignored her, clearly enjoying his fish. He opened a foil-wrapped package that had been rolled in his sleeping bag. "Trade you two pieces of chocolate cake for that potato and butter. Old Three Toes has been watching you. I'm not leaving.''

She stared at him as he placed the package on her bedroll and took the potato and butter. No one had bothered to protect her during her life, even when she was a small child. She blinked, surprised when Tyrell reached to wipe her mouth with a corner of the towel. The movement was unstudied and natural, as if he'd cared for children. She wasn't a child and no one had ever wiped her mouth. And she'd never had the large family that Tyrell had grown up in, nor the experience with children.

When she finished eating, Tyrell's dark look studied her and that quiver inside her warmed. Uncertain of herself, of what that look meant, she turned away. A tug on her hand took away her breath and she inhaled as Tyrell took her fingers to his mouth and sucked them clean, one at a time, his eyes meeting hers. Incredible sensations stormed through her, locking her body. When he took her palm, and placed his face within her keeping, kissing the center, she almost groaned. When his tongue flicked her skin, she inhaled, shivered and jerked her hand away, rubbing it against her thigh. Tyrell's rich chuckle would echo in her mind throughout the long, starlit and sleepless night. Tyrell slept deeply, his deep breathing an odd calming and safe sound not far away.

Before first light, he groaned drowsily. "Lomax, go back to sleep."

"I'm off to find the truth, Blaylock." She jerked her bootlaces into a bow and stood, rolling up her sleeping bag.

"This isn't a yellow brick road," he mumbled. He rolled on his side to study her, and his dark lazy look heated, though the morning was cold and layered with mist. "You get up early, don't you? You're probably all cheery and happy when you can ruin someone else's day."

Tyrell was grumpy in the mornings so he must like to sleep in; she tucked away that tidbit in her "Annoy-Tyrell" file. If she had to do business with him, she would do it on her terms. "Always have. There wasn't time to lie in bed. I've had to work all my life, Blaylock. I had to start young, fixing breakfast for Cutter and my father. Not all of us had cozy lives, like land grabbers. You probably had breakfast waiting on the table for you when you got up. I didn't."

"Mmm, you're right. Breakfast was always there, right after we milked the cows," he murmured thoughtfully, and turned his back to her.

She resented walking to him and prodding his backside with her boot. "What's the Three Toes situation, do you think?"

"Gone."

"How do you know?"

He grunted at her next boot-nudge. "I can't smell him. All I smell is you."

Celine tensed and wanted to fling herself upon that strong

back and shoulders turned toward her. "Are you saying I stink?"

Tyrell moved so fast, she couldn't jump free. He turned and his hand reached behind her knee; the abrupt pressure caused her legs to bend and she fell upon him.

"You're mashing me, Lomax," he teased in a dark rumble that caused her to shiver again when he was done kissing her. "Thanks for our first date. I really would like to do it again. What's for breakfast, honey?"

Four

"At least it's better than my tent." A week later, June was sweet with the scent of Jasmine's alfalfa fields and flower and vegetable gardens. Inside the vacant 1950s gas station, the air was cloaked with smells of stale oil, staler cigarette smoke, gas and dirty jokes. Lighter colored squares on the wall represented the seductive calendars she'd torn away.

Celine tore the new toilet lid from its package and set about installing herself in her first home. Just down from Mamie's Café, the hub of morning coffee breaks and Saturday night dances, the rock and concrete gas station provided a view of Jasmine's main street; it was the perfect location for Cutter Lomax's granddaughter to upset the Blaylocks' grasp on the town and the valley. Perched at one end of the street, the old gas station lacked pumps and the underground gas tanks had been removed. A long roof shot over where the pumps used to stand. The station walls were of natural rock and the plumbing still worked; stove pipes leading from the antique stoves in the front part and in the garage section remained safe. The seller was relieved to "unload…ah…I mean pass on to someone who appreciates the station's vibrant history."

He'd said that Luke Blaylock and his deputies had had a shootout with bank robbers on the site. Cutter had said he'd worked here, until the Blaylocks caused old Monty Chevaz to fire him. "It was a squeeze play, and the Blaylocks ramrodded me out of town," Cutter had said of the incident.

To uproot the Blaylocks wouldn't be a hit-and-run job and Celine needed a place to stay…and a base office from which to work. Expenses would be high and would quickly eat up the savings she needed to prove Cutter right. She wasn't worried about "making-do," surviving or earning a paycheck of some kind. She'd always managed, even as a child, to get food when Cutter and Link drank away the grocery money. As a Lomax, she had lived in far worse.

She could do any job to survive, if she couldn't ply her trade. She'd laid bricks and scrubbed floors and worked in construction, and as an adult she'd always provided for Cutter and Link. Jobs seemed to evade them as she drew better salaries.

At best, to stay in Jasmine, she could act as a temporary for other surveying companies or as a "searcher." She'd put herself through college as a "searcher" for abstract title companies, researching intensive information to confirm deeds for property sales. One visit to the courthouse had proved that her search for the truth could be lengthy. She didn't want to hire a professional abstract deed company to research—she was qualified, and the information she wanted to retrieve was old and buried. She called her old employer in Michigan, and Pete Hamstead was ready to help; he wanted her to take the time to finish whatever nagged at her and then to "Get back here. You're good, Lomax, or I wouldn't allow you to take whatever time you needed to settle this. And don't go shopping for another employer while you're off."

Pete also noted that someone was tracking her employment

and life, asking too many questions of the people who had worked with her. He asked if she needed money, or a place to hole up in. "The guy dropped by the office and was pretty sharp. He could be a private investigator. Knows his way around personnel files and legal stuff to get information. A big, tall dark guy who knows his way around numbers. Sharp and pushy and classy. Something cold about him, like he's carrying a great big hole inside. Doesn't talk much. Dora in bookkeeping said he was an Adonis. I've been sucking in my stomach for years, and she hasn't noticed. She asked him for a date and he said he was 'taken.' He's on your trail for some reason, Lomax. Watch it. Repeat—he's a big cold one."

"That would be Tyrell Blaylock and he has his moments when he is definitely as cold as an active volcano," Celine muttered. She'd expected Tyrell to dig into her past and to find her weaknesses. The Blaylock lies had covered Cutter's truth; however, her two days on the mountain had revealed none of Cutter's detailed landmarks. In the years that had passed, Cutter's trees could have been harvested, a small earthquake could dislodge or crack the stones he'd mentioned. The bluff to the east of the red cliffs could have tumbled; the edge of the forest could have advanced or receded. She'd need more than a week on the mountain with Tyrell tracing her movements.

"'Honey,' he called me. So typical of a man using soft talk to get food. I'm a woman, and I'm supposed to cook breakfast," Celine muttered, fishing into her tool chest. "The Blaylocks are not ramrodding me out of town. I bought this place so they wouldn't. It was cheaper than leasing or paying rent for the next few months, and sits square in the middle of town. It's a good place to make my stand."

She screwed the toilet lid into place and stood up. The old toilet was scrubbed clean, but the rest of the small room had layers of grime dating back to Cutter's time. Sunlight shot through the window she had replaced to reveal years of neglect. She knew the job wasn't going to be easy and that Jasmine was a tight community controlled by the Blaylocks. She'd have to question carefully, or the community wouldn't tell her anything. She'd settle in, take extra work and, on the side, make the Blaylocks her main hobby.

With a groan, Celine rubbed her aching back. She walked into the big front room, a perfect place for her new office. Celine didn't want to think about the garage at the back of the building, cluttered with junk and rubble. She'd go through every bit of it, seeing if there was anything she could use or trade, before discarding the rest.

She eyed the water dripping from the ceiling into a battered bucket, and groaned again. Pete Hamstead wouldn't like watermarked surveys. She went outside, hauled out a ladder she'd found and placed it against the building, hefting her toolbox up with her. Once the building was solid, she'd take a day to go to a town that had a thrift shop and buy necessities, like a bed.

She hefted the toolbox onto the roof and crawled onto the steeplelike surface, which would need reshingling before winter. Celine let out one more groan and looked down the street. This was the town that Cutter claimed had turned against him because of Luke Blaylock and Boone Llewlyn's lies. *Why hadn't she found just one of the landmarks Cutter had raved about placing on the mountain?* Where was the "big house" he'd built in a canyon on Lomax land?

Tyrell ripped the plane down the rough board. He scowled at old Three Toes who sat a distance away, watching. Three Toes liked honey and women, and he'd almost strolled into Celine's camp to sniff and rub against her like a big pet. For selfish reasons, Tyrell did not want to share Celine with the bear, or anyone else.

In the week and a half since he watched her walk down the mountain trail, pulling her little red wagon behind her, he'd done a lot of thinking. Her words haunted him— "There

wasn't time to lie in bed. I've had to work all my life, Blaylock.
I had to start young, fixing breakfast for Cutter and my father.
Not all of us had cozy lives. You probably had breakfast wait-
ing on the table for you when you got up. I didn't.''

He'd had a perfect boyhood, filled with warm clothing, nu-
tritious food and love. And he'd walked away. He'd never forget his father's last phone call, the ache in it, a father wanting
his son. He should have come back—to see his family was too
painful now.

Mason's and Hillary's lack of confidence in him underlined
how Tyrell had misplaced his life's goals.

He ripped the plane down the board again, watching the curl
of wood fall gracefully into the pile at his feet. He had no idea
why Celine Lomax excited and haunted him, why he felt new
just looking at her and delighted by the temper in her dark
green eyes. Tyrell inhaled the fresh mountain air, blended with
the scent of his morning coffee and the planed wood. He really
needed to fell trees today, not think of Celine's soft body, or
that curious, softening touch of her hand upon his nape.

She'd be hurt…when she found the truth, that Cutter had
lied. That she'd based her career and life on that lie. She'd had
enough pain in her life, and was in for more. He wanted to
protect her and had no idea why. But he would protect his
family. Tyrell swore abruptly, the words rich and dark; they
startled Three Toes who was sitting at the edge of the forest,
watching him.

Tyrell settled down to wallow in his dark mood, one created
by a woman his body and mind craved. A woman who wanted
to take away his family land. Very quietly, so as not to upset
his family, Tyrell had researched the legal descriptions of land
and deeds and transfers. Until Celine uncovered contradictory
information, the Blaylock homestead had been legally acquired
and had always been in their family. As a matter of legal record, Cutter had committed robberies in other towns.

Tyrell wanted to protect her, to cuddle her, to haul all that passionate full-bodied woman into his arms and make love to her. He didn't like his lack of control near Celine Lomax, nor his hunger for her now.

He cursed again, startling Three Toes, just a cub when Rio had rescued him from a trap. The bear who loved cookies and women ran off into the pines, meeting and passing Celine.

Scowling at Tyrell and in a high temper, Celine disregarded the fleeing bear. She made her way toward Tyrell. "You!" she shouted, her breasts quivering beneath the light T-shirt with every step. "You are making my life miserable, Blaylock!"

Tyrell stopped planing in midsweep, jolted by the sight of her feminine curves beneath the light cloth. Celine wasn't overflowing and she wasn't slight; she was just right and there was enough flare to those hips to— Withholding the desire that leaped upon him whenever he thought about Celine's body in his hands, he forced himself to continue planing slowly down the board. He had an odd sense that if Celine's passion ran to sensual and not to high temper, he would not stand a chance. He remembered that missing button, and the glimpse of creamy skin beneath it. The volatile woman striding toward him, vibrant curls flying, green eyes blazing, had enough passion to tear a dead man from his grave. Tyrell tried to be disgusted by the light-feeling glow within him, by the excitement skittering through his body, and failed.

He purposefully ignored Celine, who reacted as he knew she would—she hit him on his bare back with two open hands. He put down his plane and turned to her, pushing away the smile on his face. "Lay off," he said simply, knowing it would set her off even more.

"Lay off, yourself. You've been digging in my life, foraging for bills owed and dark, dirty secrets. You didn't find them, did you? I owe no one, Blaylock. You can't get your nasty hands on my life that way. I'm one hundred percent debt-free. So, knowing you couldn't get to me that way, you sent your family after me."

"What?" Tyrell tensed; he didn't want his family involved with Celine's quest. Link, her father, had once returned to town with the same quest and things got nasty. But then Link wasn't sweet and neither was Tyrell's father, not when his wife had been insulted.

"Oh, fine. The innocent act. You told them to come all at once, didn't you, bringing all those lovely children, to clean my gas station. You wanted me obligated to the Blaylocks, so you put them up to bringing in household family stuff, a refrigerator, that lovely old bed and table, and all the rest. They gave me this baby to hold, Roman and Kallista's little toddler and he wouldn't let me go—he hugged me. Then he went to sleep in my arms and I didn't know what to do. It happened so fast, and they wouldn't listen, and now thanks to you, I've got a refrigerator full of food, no mice, the walls scrubbed clean and plenty of obligations to your family... Well, I'm not grateful."

"That's what they do, Lomax. For anyone who is new and needs a helping hand. They're a family who likes to help. You don't owe them anything. Did anyone say you did? Did they ask you for anything?" Tyrell watched that soak in, Celine's eyes widening slowly, her face paling beneath the freckles. He touched those on the tip of her nose. "Did Else bring apple pie? She uses my mother's recipe."

"She did. Approximately twelve inches in diameter. Lattice top, sprinkled with sugar. A big, high, flaky crust, apple pie with butter and cinnamon," Celine replied in a sinking, dull tone. "They all asked me to dinner. I don't take handouts and I didn't have a chance, and you knew it. You deliberately set them upon me."

"It's called a family and a neighborly thing to do," Tyrell murmured gently, smoothing back the curl that brushed her temple. His thumb stayed to brush that silky skin, the pulse beating strong beneath it. Just like his mother, no one could stop Else if she thought a neighbor needed help. He'd helped neighbors before leaving Jasmine and helping people gave more than it took. It had been a long time since he'd felt good about helping anyone.

He wanted to draw Celine against him and hold her, protect her from what she would discover about his family and her own. He'd grown up in a loving community, and had been protected from life; Celine hadn't. "You'd better go home now, Celine Lomax, and cool down. Because if you don't, I'm going to kiss you and you're going to kiss me back," Tyrell said as gently as he could.

She looked up at him, scowled and said, "Before I get really mad, and take you apart, I'm supposed to tell you that Kallista is expecting again, and the due date agrees with Paloma and Rio's... The whole family seemed to delight in telling me that, one at a time... I don't know why, I'm not a family sort— Now back to you, Blaylock. You're threatening me. That's just typical. I expected it."

Tyrell looked down at her face and thought of his brothers, how the Blaylocks were meant to be family men, how babies were loved and cherished, and how much he wanted Celine.

"Expect this, Lomax," Tyrell said a heartbeat before he tugged her into his arms. His mouth held lightning bolts when it came down, fusing to hers, and stunning her until she couldn't move. The seductive aftershocks bolted her boots to the spring earth. She reached for balance and found warm, smooth skin, muscles rippling beneath her fingers. She pushed her mouth against his, not wanting him to get ahead of her in this strange fascinating play. His tongue flicked along her lips and nudged entrance into her mouth. He tasted like a dark rich journey she had to take, her body heating for the pleasure. He suckled her tongue as she kept up her end of the contest, and the most unique ecstasy shivered its way through her, heating and jolting cords low in her body. She clamped her arms around him, not letting him escape before she was finished.

With a low dark groan, Tyrell shook within her grasp and slid his big hand to cover her breast.

Stunned by the caress, she stood still looking up at him. Tyrell's expression had darkened. As his fingers smoothed her so gently, she cried out, clinging to him because her legs had gone weak. Still dazed, she didn't stand a chance when he lifted her slowly, to place his mouth upon her breast, suckling her gently through her clothing. The image of his dark head against her breast jarred her. He seemed so vulnerable then, his big body tensed. He groaned shakily when her hands pressed against his head, drawing him nearer.

She'd wanted him. Tyrell's big body quivered against hers, and the incredible gentle touch of his hands cradled her face. He stood perfectly still as she traced his sleek eyebrows, and, for just a moment, she knew he waited for her touch, that she had the power to— Celine's eyes widened as the knowledge stunned her. For just that moment, Tyrell needed her touch, waited for it. He was rather sweet, all flushed and warm and waiting for her fingertips to travel over his face, exploring him.

Whatever this magnificent creature was, resting and tethered beneath her touch, he wouldn't be careless of her. Her instincts told her that Tyrell would do a very thorough job of arousing her, of seeing to her pleasure before his own.

Then his eyes blazed down on her, his scowl dark and furious. "Get out of my life, Lomax, before something happens that we'll both regret."

"I'm not regretting anything. I'm taking him down." Celine propped her boots up on her empty desk and tapped her pen on the blank yellow pad. She drew a big zero on the page to represent her cash flow. She resented taking anything from the Blaylocks, especially the lovely old bed, dresser and dining table. She'd loved polishing them, watching the wood glow to life after years in storage. The bedroom set, a carved walnut four-poster and dresser, was beautiful. The antique table with spool legs matched a buffet and the well-used rocker creaked almost musically.

She'd return all the furniture, of course, with payment for its use. She tapped her pen on the ad she had just placed in Jasmine's newspaper last week. No one had answered it, but property usually sold in the spring and the fall, not the third week of June. The poster she'd painted and taped to the station's big window mocked her—Temporary Office For Lomax Surveying. She'd added Fees Negotiable after the first week without customers.

Picking up work at the courthouse by checking abstracts furnished small financial relief, but not enough. She scanned a copy of the notice she'd plastered on every store bulletin board she could find—Lomax Surveying. Experienced Surveyor And Abstract Searcher. Fees Negotiable.

The telephone on the scarred wooden desk was one the newspaper had traded for her article, "Women in Traditional Men's Jobs." She'd take any work to fund reclaiming Lomax land; she was prepared to stay until every suspect foot and marker had been surveyed.

While Tyrell had the luxury of holing up on his mountain lair, she did not have the luxury of waiting. She was getting really tired of eating pancakes morning, noon and night, hot and cold and always without butter. If she didn't get a customer soon, she'd have to get a message machine for her office and find work elsewhere. Work in small towns like Jasmine ran to farm labor and clerking. She'd done both; she could again.

She'd created a little makeshift home as she'd always done, stuffing blue fruit jars with wildflowers and using discarded thrift cotton sheets to make curtains. She loved sleeping in that grand antique bedroom set, four posters all carved and the glass flower drawer knobs blue with age. "Just an old thing propped up in the barn. We won't miss it, and I'd really like to think of you sleeping in our grandparents' bed. That's a quilt our grandmother made with bits of shirts and leftovers for her hope

chest. Girls don't have hope chests now, a chest to put what
they'd made for their future homes, but they should. I did and
dreamed of my sweetheart with each stitch," Else had said with
a hug.

A hug. Unfamiliar with the expression of affection, Celine
had stiffened within Else's embrace. She'd turned to protesting
the Blaylock men hard at work on laying new flooring over
that concrete floor in the back garage. She'd found herself
picked up and tossed from one to the other and out the door—
it shut firmly behind her. While Else was busy juggling huge
pots of food on the station's tiny gas stove, the Blaylock wives
had been hard at work scrubbing, wallpapering and teasing
each other. Else's husband, Joe, had come up behind his wife
and kissed the side of her neck. A grandmother several times
over, Else had squealed in delight and had turned to sneak a
fond pat on Joe's lean bottom.

It had been just too much, a happy family at work. How
would they feel about that when she took part of their land
away and cleared Cutter's reputation? The sweet little toddler
that she'd held, Roman and Kallista's Kipp, could be hurt. Celine didn't like feeling guilty; she'd never done anything to
hurt anyone in her lifetime.

Celine tapped her pen. She didn't want to worry about the
Blaylocks and their problems. She had her own. Getting jobs
was one of them and blushing every time she thought of Tyrell's kiss was another.

Celine sucked in her breath and knew she'd just blushed
again. She blushed every time she thought about Tyrell's hand
on her breast, the way her body responded to him. Cutter had
made sex sound ugly and she knew the mechanics and the pain,
yet she wasn't prepared for the beauty of simple, gentle
touches, of light brushing kisses that enticed. Then there was
that dark gentle biting thing that sucked her breath away and
caused her heart to leap.

"Oh, he'd know all about that, I suppose, how to melt a

woman down to her work boots," Celine muttered as she watched a tall man wearing an expensive three-piece suit stride toward her office. Tanned to perfection, the man's dark well-groomed hair ran in waves to his shoulders. He carried a small colorful florist's bouquet, and Celine liked the romantic thought of him taking flowers to a woman when his business was done at Lomax Surveying. To appear as if she had work, Celine hurried to scribble notes on a pad, tore them free and scattered them near the telephone. She reached into the desk drawer and whopped a stack of clean paper on her desk, scribbled on the top page, and turned to check on her framed college degree. She badly needed work to finance her own quest. "Come and get it. I'll survey anything you want and boy, will it cost," she whispered, almost feeling cash in her palm.

The man looked expensive and talked in a soft, liquid Southern drawl. "Miss Lomax, I'm Channing Boudreaux, the Third, Kallista's former employer and friend." He scanned the rough desk left from the gas station days and the barren room, her surveyor's transit carefully packed and tripods propped against a corner. "I thought you might like these to brighten up your new office."

He handed her the gay multicolored carnation bouquet and while Celine tried to close her gaping mouth, Channing took her hand and lifted it to his lips, kissing the back. "You're every bit as lovely as they said you were, Miss Lomax. I wonder if I might have the pleasure of—"

Celine stared at Tyrell, who had just stepped into her office and had leaned back against a wall. He wore a work shirt, worn jeans and his moccasins, and he had shaved. Though his blue-black hair still brushed his shoulders, he looked just as he had in New York, very tough and lean, a steel-coated numbers-knight. The chambray shirt, open at the throat, stretched across his rangy shoulders, and Celine's fingers itched to smooth the small wedge of hair on his chest. She felt the concrete floor vibrate beneath her boots and her temperature rise in the cool room; that little quiver around her heart was probably anger and once she caught her breath, she'd—

He crossed his arms and something in the dark, grim way he looked at her, down at her hand in Channing's and then at Channing, set her off. She felt guilty for no reason, but she jerked her hand away from Channing's. "What do you want, Blaylock?"

The two tall men looked at each other, and Celine grasped the edge of her desk. Evidently gauging each other, the men smiled coldly, one elegant and sophisticated and the other dark and broody, as if his kingdom had been invaded. "Tyrell, I presume," Channing said, as the men shook hands in a brief manner that challenged.

Celine had seen males flexing their muscles, sizing each other up, and now the ritual fascinated her. She leaned forward to study the men; from her other experiences, working with men who argued over women, there had to be a woman involved. She frowned; she didn't want to think of Tyrell and another woman.

Tyrell shot her a dark, warning glance that sizzled and set her thinking of his kiss, of her kissing him back. Celine straightened; Tyrell had just warned her that other men were off limits. She wasn't certain how she liked the possessive trait, with her as a possession. In business, he was known for his exact, thorough technique; apparently that extended to other aspects of his life. Celine pushed away the little tingle of guilt he'd created, as if she'd been unfaithful, and glared at him. Seemingly satisfied that he had made his point, Tyrell turned to Channing and nodded. "Boudreaux," he returned coolly.

"One doesn't often hear of you coming down from your mountain, Tyrell," Channing said smoothly, easing his well-clad hip onto Celine's desk as if preparing to stay. "You came down for winter supplies and then you came down to dump Miss Lomax on Else's doorstep. I understand Miss Lomax has a mind of her own, and I like that in a woman."

Channing smiled warmly, intimately at Celine as if she interested him. Uncertain of how to react, and off balance at the very first male who was openly flirting with her, she smiled tentatively back at him. Because she was nervous, she twirled her finger in a curl. She liked Channing, despite his expensive exterior. Channing's grin deepened. "That's a lovely dimple, you have there, Miss Lomax. Simply enchanting."

"Her dimple isn't your business, Channing. I have business with Miss Lomax," Tyrell stated smoothly in a low, cool tone.

Celine blinked, trying to understand the meanings swirling beneath the words. They escaped her. She had images of raised fur and almost heard growling sounds and had no idea why the two men were at odds when they'd just met. Just then, a blond woman, wearing a tight pink sweater, tighter pants and high heels flounced into the small office.

"Tyrell!" the blond squealed. "I'm so glad you're back! I would have come up on your mountain to bring you something delicious—my lasagna is famous, you know. But goodness, no woman could possibly make it up that rough mountain trail. You can't just hoard yourself away like that."

She hurried to Tyrell, her heavy perfume filling the air, and hurled herself at him, her lips pouted for a kiss. Something hot and dangerous slithered through Celine—she wanted to tear the woman away from Tyrell. She looked at the paper she had just crumpled in her fist. She shivered, thinking about how her grandfather had spoken of Garnet Marie, how he wanted to pry Luke Blaylock away from her.

Tyrell held the woman a distance away, his smile cool as he turned her toward Channing. "Lettie, you're just as lovely as ever. I'm afraid I'm out of a job and not many prospects in sight— Meet Channing Boudreaux the Third. He visits Jasmine once in a while, but he travels all over the world. He's rich and he's single."

"Oh...too bad you don't have a job, Tyrell. Jasmine really doesn't have much call for high-powered executives." Like a hawk spying juicy new prey, Lettie leaned toward Channing. She breathed deeply and the low cut of her sweater filled with her breasts. She toyed with a curl of her blond hair and licked her lips. "You're the man who stays at Roman's old house sometimes, aren't you? The owner of a string of fancy resorts? Kallista's friend?"

Channing's look at Tyrell could have cut steel. "I am," he said politely in his Southern drawl. Celine noted the layers of frost.

"He just said he was looking for someone to have lunch with him," Tyrell murmured, sliding a dark warning glance at Celine. She could feel a future paycheck slip away from her as Tyrell derailed her first client.

"*Ohh!* I'm just hungry as a big bad bear," Lettie cooed, wrapping her arms around Channing's arm. She fluttered her lashes up at him. "Shall we go?"

"Wait! Channing…I mean Mr. Boudreaux. Did you have business you wanted to discuss?" Celine asked, hearing her own desperation.

"I do indeed," Channing murmured, and flicked a cold stare at Tyrell before Lettie dragged him down the street to Mamie's Café.

"Now, look what you've done, Blaylock. You ran off my first client deliberately—" Celine stopped talking when Tyrell began walking toward her. She recognized that dark, sultry, taut look and her heart seemed to quiver and leap within her. She backed up against the wall as he placed a hand on either side of her head, caging her body with his. "Don't you bite me, Blaylock," she whispered.

"I'd like to nibble on you all over… Channing is very experienced. You're not," he said, brushing his lips against hers as his fingers toyed with her hair.

"You dug in my life. You know I'm experienced. I've worked for years as a surveyor and—"

His lips brushed hers again. "It's been three weeks. Did you miss me?"

The question was husky and raw, as if he'd hated asking, but needed the answer. His dark eyes searched her face and he seemed almost vulnerable, waiting for her answer. Celine looked away, wishing she had more skill to cover her emotions. She ached for him to touch her breast, to hold it as he would a treasure. Celine had not been treasured in her lifetime—except for her high quality work.

"You're blushing, sweetheart," he whispered gently against her ear.

"What do you want?" she whispered back as every part of her body shook with the need to taste his hard magical mouth. "Did you want her?" she had to ask, whispering in his ear.

"I have never wanted a woman in my life like I want you," he answered firmly. "And that's the poor, sad truth of it," he added before he reached down to lift her up into his arms.

He sat in her desk chair with Celine on his lap and studied her with amused interest. "What's wrong? You look as if you're going to explode."

"You can't just come out and say things like that."

His black brows rose. "I want you and that is a fact, Miss Celine Lomax. I'd prefer you didn't complicate matters by encouraging Channing. He's almost family by way of Kallista, my sister-in-law."

"Me? Encourage him? How? I mean, I need the work, but—" The idea suddenly hit her; she turned it slowly around, examining the possibility that Channing found her "enchanting." "He would have rather stayed here than go with Lettie, wouldn't he? Why, how nice of him. You know, he appears to be such a gentleman."

"Hah," Tyrell exclaimed abruptly, drawing her closer. He took her face in his large hands, cradling it for his inspection. She saw herself in his black eyes. He took away her glasses, tossing them to her desk. She knew he wanted something from her, needing something, and the incredible sorrow that flickered in his eyes just that moment caused her to reach out her hand and place it on his cheek. He closed his eyes, those long glossy lashes gleaming against his dark skin, his head tilting slowly to rest against her palm. "It's been a long three weeks, Celine."

"What is it you need, Tyrell?" she whispered. She had worked with men who had lost wives and children; she'd seen the haunted lost look, recognized it now in Tyrell and knew that he carried deep, secret sorrow.

He slowly pulled her closer, to rest her cheek against his. She sensed his incredible sadness and, for the moment, allowed him to hold her. "You're not alone," she whispered, because being alone was the worst thing in the world. "You have your family."

He tensed, placed a quick rough kiss on her cheek and stood up with her in his arms. He slowly released her and walked to the window, placing his back to her, his hands jammed in his back pockets, his legs braced apart. "You're staying then."

His tone was too ominous and stormy as if he fought something within himself.

What had happened just then? Why had she reached out to Tyrell? And why had whatever darkness within him settled at her touch?

He turned quickly, reminding her of that cold steely man in New York, who knew exactly what he wanted and how to get it. "I need office space. I'd like to rent from you. The location here is good, easy to reach."

Celine plopped into the chair still warm from Tyrell's body. She stood up. "Sure, and I can see you tramping up and down that mountain every day. I'm not taking charity, Blaylock. Neither am I being bought off. If you want to keep tabs on me—"

"Lay off, Lomax. I've decided to go back into business...here in Jasmine, as a financial consultant and investment manager. My former colleagues at Mason's have decided to

start their own business. They never believed the worst of me—
a condition created by someone we both know. I've agreed to
be their off-site consultant. Else won't mind me bunking at the
old place—at her house—during the work week. And I want
to help Rio at his remodeled home when I can. I wouldn't want
to intrude on my newly married brother's privacy and I'll sleep
in his barn. I'll spend the weekends at the cabin.''

She needed money desperately. She'd have to rent to him.
''I'll think about it,'' she said slowly, not wanting to appear
too eager. She knew Cutter would turn over in his grave, raging
at her for sharing anything with a Blaylock.

Weighing his offer against her pride, she had to be practical;
she couldn't refuse Tyrell's rent money. ''Maybe, I'll think
about it,'' she corrected, not wanting to let him get his way
easily.

Tyrell's expression reminded her of when she'd first seen
him—all brisk business, impatient with any delays; she decided
that she enjoyed delaying Tyrell. He leaned closer. ''Good, you
do that. And I'd like to hire you. If you're going to be surveying my property, you might as well get paid for it. I want an
updated survey.''

She curled her hand into a fist and wanted to punch him. He
knew she didn't have other prospects, that he would be her
only client—a Blaylock. ''You're down on your luck now,
Blaylock. You'll have to pay up front. I'll want a contract and
I work by the hour. You might not like the fee and then I'd
have to take you to court. You might not like what I might
find. Then I'm going to take what I've found to prove my
grandfather right, and I'm going straight to an attorney with
enough evidence to rip away your land. If I have to do two
surveys, one for you and one for my purposes to keep legal, I
will. I'm very thorough and since I'm working alone, the survey will take a long time. A very long time. I charge for equipment and by the hour.''

''I'd expect a contract—your name and mine on the same

legal document, Lomax and Blaylock. And I'll want a not-to-exceed a certain time limit clause. According to my sources, you are very good, especially in field work.... About my office space, I'll need a proper business sign. I won't charge for adding your name. You might think about deducting a portion of the rent for the use of the office equipment I'll have to have,'' Tyrell said, scanning the barren office she had created. Her worn topographical maps lay neatly stacked on a table, her engineering scale placed over a supply of onion skin paper and transparent plastic sheets; fresh pencils stuffed into an old chipped mug. A new surveyor's field book, where all legal, monument and other descriptions would be written was on her scarred desk—Blaylock had been printed across it in big, black bold letters and retraced several times.

He frowned at Channing's bouquet, which Celine had just picked up to place in water. Then her only client and a Blaylock walked out the door, leaving her shaking without knowing why.

Five

With the air of a man who lived alone and liked silence, Tyrell tilted his head to one side. As he had for the past week and a half, he noted the unique sound of an approaching engine with a certain hiccup. On an early July night, Jasmine's streets were quiet as Celine's battered pickup pulled up beside the gas station and died with a sputtering cough. She'd been researching Blaylock land descriptions at the courthouse again, some seventy miles away. A perfectionist, she wanted all the details in a row before planning her assault on Blaylock land. Her pickup's bald tires could have caused an accident on the curving, mountainous road where his parents had died. Tyrell eased back into his desk chair, relieved that she was safe.

He should have been in Jasmine, waiting to see if his parents had arrived safely from their trip to Cheyenne. The rest of his siblings had been concerned about his parents, but Tyrell had been worrying about the financial intricacies of a merger. He rubbed the familiar burning ache in his stomach, one he'd gotten in the high stress lane of Mason Diversified.

Celine had driven a hard bargain, and her acceptance of his offer was less than gracious. "Okay, we both know I need the money. Do not touch anything on my side of the room and I expect payment in advance. I'll make a list and if you cross any one of the defined rules, I'll evict you. I'd like that, evicting a down-and-out hotshot like you. I'm glad that you are having to face the world and work for a living," she had ended in one of those beautiful smirks. "One bad check and I'll prosecute."

Tyrell pushed his hands through his hair and admitted that nothing had stirred him in his lifetime like Celine. He was in a state of delicate unbalance and he was feeling…delicate. A controlled man with meticulous habits, he placed his pencil neatly in the black plastic container on his new desk. Since Celine had agreed to rent him office space, he'd set about nudging his way into her life; he knew about infiltration and take-overs. He did not enjoy this past week of staying in Rio's barn.

Tyrell had ordered office furniture immediately, with a high delivery cost. Matching bookshelves and desk had arrived with file cabinets, a copier, a computer and supplies. Contrasting Celine's side of the office with battered topographical maps and old equipment, his space was neatly organized, sleek and new. To make her more comfortable with sharing her life and space, he'd deliberately chosen less than top-of-the-line brands—except his new laptop computer and calculator, both equipped with extra batteries for work at the cabin. He neatly stacked his research on shifting aggressive and dangerous stock investments into safer ones for the elderly Minos couple. Edna and Frank had walked into his office just as he was folding Celine's clothes, fresh from the new washer-dryer set. "I've always trusted a man who does laundry and who irons," Edna had said, glancing at his brand new ironing board and the Super Gizmo Iron.

He loved that iron, and he liked taking care of Celine. The pleasures of housekeeping had surprised him, though Celine had quickly made a home in the garage, filling it with colorful odd curtains and seashells brimming with aromatic herbs.

He placed the file in a neatly arranged drawer, just as his life had been before Celine had entered it. He enjoyed the familiar work, digging at potential earnings, looking at disposable assets and calculating financial risks and profits. He enjoyed helping the elderly retired people who feared for their savings.

This morning, his brothers and he had installed the washer and dryer in the garage. Roman and James had argued about the placement of the four-legged, old-fashioned bathtub with a circular shower curtain. After a heated discussion, they had installed the bathtub and new water heater into one corner and built a wall, enclosing the tub for privacy. They'd always worked together, and Tyrell had missed the friendly elbow jabs, the older brother threats and taunts. He'd missed his brothers and Else, the love and memories that surrounded them. But it wasn't that easy to forgive himself for not coming back sooner; his father's last telephone call still haunted him.

Celine's pickup door slammed and Tyrell ran his hand down his smoothly shaven cheek. She seemed to like the well-trimmed Channing Boudreaux. Jasmine's barber had enjoyed cutting the length from Tyrell's hair, leaving it to just touch his shirt collar.

Neil Morris, the local bachelor veterinarian, had dropped by to check out the new woman in Jasmine. After a brief conversation with Tyrell, he was disgusted with the Blaylock sons for snapping up all the "prime bride stock." Neil wasn't too certain he was giving up to Tyrell. He hadn't even met the new surveyor yet.

After Neil finally left, Tyrell went grocery shopping and stocked the tiny kitchenette against one wall of the garage. On a whim, he'd purchased two perfect candles and glass holders, placing them on a sturdy, but old table that had come from Blaylock storage. He'd enjoyed steaming broccoli and braising mushrooms, garlic and onion and preparing a fettuccine sauce.

While the washer and dryer were humming with Celine's clothes, he'd washed the romaine lettuce for salad. He couldn't wait to see Celine eat a proper dinner, instead of munching on a cold rolled-up pancake.

Through the window, he studied Celine's tired expression and her slumped shoulders. He did not enjoy watching Celine drive herself to death, trying to substantiate Cutter's lies. On Celine's desk, Channing's wilted bouquet taunted Tyrell. He rose to open the door for her and she dragged by without looking at him.

"Something smells. Lock up when you leave," she muttered, carrying a cardboard box marked Thrift Shop under her arm. She plopped her baseball cap and backpack on her desk and trudged back to the old garage. She shut the door between them. The click of the lock she'd installed that morning said she'd protected herself for a long time. She'd had to; the Lomaxes had lived in tough neighborhoods.

"So much for appreciation of coming home to a hot meal and a bath," Tyrell murmured dryly. When Celine did not answer his light knock at the door, he sighed. He wondered when he'd last had a good comforting beer buzz and when Celine's temper would ignite.

Tyrell smiled. He really looked forward to Celine discovering the new washer and dryer, the bathtub and the meal he'd cooked. She wouldn't like his interference, but then he didn't like her lugging laundry to The Wash House when she was half dead from working. He waited a moment more, then decided to see if the tavern side of Mamie's Café still had that old jukebox and if the pool table still had that neat little hollow that made balls curve into the pocket.

Late the next afternoon, Tyrell fought the remainders of a dull headache; he hadn't experienced the potent aftermath of a boys' night out since his teenage days. He'd always been too controlled after those first few tests. The Western hat that Else had plopped on his head didn't feel quite as tight as it had at dawn, when she'd found him sleeping on her front porch. She'd ripped the towel away from his eyes with all the tenderness of Godzilla; she'd grinned as the rising sun bored a burning hole through his throbbing head. His groan brought laughter and a glass of icy water over his head. "She's got to you, hasn't she? I knew it would happen someday and not with a bloodless witch like the one you almost married. When you brought her home last year—well, it's better off left unsaid. If you want butter on your pancakes, Mr. Lazybones, get out and milk the cows."

The porch had been added onto the original Blaylock homestead cabin, which was now a comfortable family room for Else's grandchildren to play. Tyrell had grown up on the family ranch now owned by his sister, and home seemed a good place to come when the earth was reeling. Neil hadn't been quite so disgruntled about losing "another female to the Blaylocks" when they ended the session at two o'clock. Neil and Tyrell found they had a common problem: ladies' man Channing Boudreaux. Then Channing had dropped in and a friendly match-you-beer-for-beer contest followed, providing a hefty morning hangover.

As the first of July heat simmered over the pastures, Tyrell glanced at his brothers. He'd been helping them straighten posts and tighten barbed wire that Dan and Hannah's buffalo bull had just walked through. Big Al was a throwback and didn't like fences. Rio's Corriente bull was acting up in the field bordering Else and Joe's spread and on an opposite corner, Boone's Hereford bull snorted challenges. When one of the Blaylocks had trouble, they all pitched in to help and despite his hangover this morning, Tyrell had enjoyed working with his brothers again. He'd forgotten how it was to work on a ranch, baling hay with Joe at dawn and drinking Else's lemonade from a fruit jar at noon.

He scanned the valley, a patchwork of green fields. He'd grown up here, but it was the wild roses of the mountains that he loved, the wild call that settled a need within him. As a boy, he'd speared fish, and he'd learned to hunt with his father, brothers and Else. He'd torn berry branches away from their bush and had camped by himself as soon as his parents would agree. Swimming naked in the icy lake surrounded by aspens and cottonwood trees had been his solace; too soon he felt numbers moving inside him, prodding him, and then the offers for scholarships arrived and the world outside of Jasmine beckoned him.

He inhaled the scent of the freshly baled hay and watched a covey of quail soar out of the sagebrush. Organizing her assault on his land, Celine would be fighting her battles, burning herself down to nothing, trying to find truth in Cutter's lie. Tyrell smiled—or she could be hunting him. Celine wouldn't like his interference in her life, or the new appliances; she wasn't happy when the Blaylocks had dropped in to help her. She didn't trust the Blaylocks and she would find suspicion in his reasons for installing the washer and dryer and the tub. She'd probably hate Tyrell's roses, seeing them as a buy-off. He found himself thinking that she looked like a tiny little sweet rosebud herself, that morning he'd watched her sleep on the mountain.

Just then, Roman's Herefords pushed through a section of damaged fence and cows and calves rushed for freedom. His brothers leveled stares at him. No words were needed; their expressions said it was his turn to play roundup.

"Cinnamon," James's big saddlebred gelding, moved smoothly beneath Tyrell as he followed the small herd, the old skills of riding and herding coming back to him. He hadn't felt as free for a long time. Everything had been here—why hadn't he seen it then?

"Not everything." He looked at the battered pickup eating up the dirt road to the ranch and knew life couldn't be better— Celine would be all fired up and wanting to tangle, her green eyes lashing at him, her color high. There wasn't a drop of cold in her; passion ran through her like a tumbling lava river.

He truly looked forward to seeing her again. She wouldn't like those little tidbits he'd dropped on Neil and Channing during their beerfest.

Celine's brakes squealed to a stop by the Blaylock men who were repairing damaged fences. One tire started an angry hiss. Instantly the pickup's left front end began to slant down. She was tired and she'd lost an entire day, hunting Tyrell.

He was hiding of course, after drinking beer and telling Neil Morris and Channing that she was "spoken for." They had told her that, despite her contrary temperament, Tyrell had elegantly phrased his decision "to court the lovely flower of my life for the purpose of holy matrimony."

Dressed in a T-shirt and her cutoff shorts and work boots, "the lovely flower" of Tyrell's life rounded the pickup and marched toward the men with murder on her mind. The Blaylock brothers straightened, all in a row, tall rugged men with tanned skin and black sleek hair that gleamed in the sun. Lined up without their shirts, and wearing jeans, Western hats and boots, the Blaylocks were a heart-stopping masculine buffet as they smiled at her. Towering over her, each one promptly took off his hat and greeted her. "Miss Lomax. My wife has been asking about you," James said.

"Hannah wants to know if you can come to dinner," Dan said with a grin.

"Well, I..." She didn't want to become friends with the Blaylocks; she hadn't needed friends in her lifetime—Cutter and Link's mobile lifestyle, escaping bill collectors, hadn't left time. She swallowed and blurted out, "I want to see the baby. Do you know where he is?"

Logan frowned. "'The baby'?"

"Yes, your little brother. He's causing trouble and I'm ending it."

"Tyrell?" Roman asked with a frown. "Causing trouble?"

"Not Tyrell," Dan said firmly. "Mr. Cool and Order in

Numbers? He's just about as righteous as it gets. He always goes by the book.''

"Stop defending him.'' Celine kicked the dusty road with her boot, and folded her arms across her chest. She leveled her darkest stare at them. ''He's not innocent. He's not cool. He's a hit-and-run artist. He knows I can't afford those new appliances you helped him install. Oh, yes, I heard all about it from the newspaper clerk, who saw everything—all of you were there. Do not protect him. Nothing will keep me from killing him.''

"Man, I'd like to see this,'' Rio said with a grin.

"He's messing in my life.'' The image of the Westerner riding the big reddish brown horse over the hill caused Celine to suck in her breath. His hair caught the wind, swept back from his hard face, all angles and planes, and dark stubble covered his jaw. His shoulders gleamed in the July sunlight, the muscles on his arms flexing as he reined the horse. His legs tightened on the horse and Celine's whole body went taut, almost feeling him move against her.

She couldn't be distracted; Tyrell had interfered once more in her life. She leveled another stare at the Blaylocks. ''Do not interfere. Do not protect him.''

She leveled her anger at the man who had just drawn the big horse to stop. ''You know I can't afford that washer and dryer, Blaylock,'' she shot at him.

Tyrell slid smoothly from the saddle, grinned at her and vaulted smoothly over the fence. He moved as if nothing could stop him from taking her in his arms. ''Miss me?'' he asked huskily before lowering his lips to hers.

Celine blinked once before his mouth fused to hers and her intent to kill him strolled out into the July sunshine. She locked her fingertips to his warm bare skin and held onto the swirling, magical heat that seemed to lift her feet off the ground.

Tyrell slowly eased his lips from hers and after a dazed moment, Celine realized that her feet were actually off the ground.

"Hi, honey," he whispered in a deep, intimate tone that jarred every nerve in her body.

"Hi," she heard herself whisper huskily.

"How was your day?" he asked as if she'd just come home to him.

"Fine—" Suddenly she remembered that she'd come to kill him. She kicked Tyrell's shin and he grunted, lowering her. His muscles rippled and dark skin gleamed as he bent to rub his leg briefly. He straightened and lazily flicked a curl along her temple, testing her. She tried to talk, but the gleaming width of his shoulders barred all thought. That wedge of hair on his chest beckoned her fingertips, and his flat stomach slid down to the waistband of his jeans, which had slipped a bit off his hips. Then there was more of him, all hard angles and gleaming sunlit skin, and she remembered how he had felt, aroused and lying within the cradle of her legs, his back rippling beneath her palms. She squeezed her lids shut to close Tyrell Blaylock from her. If she didn't, she'd leap upon him and—

Tyrell bent to playfully nuzzle her neck with a growl. Startled, she couldn't move until he gently nipped her skin. Then she jumped. She knew how to lock heat and cold outside her body, but she couldn't stop the electric jolt of that intimate caress.

She shivered and tried to ignore the fingertip prowling along her lashes. She glanced at the other brothers lined up against the fence, all wearing just their jeans, boots and leather gloves with their Western hats tipped back on their heads. They watched with interest as their youngest brother bent to tie her bootlaces. "Don't do that. I'm mad at you."

"I like taking care of you."

She saw her hand stretched to smooth his rippling back—to feel all that heat and power and mystery, so close and so enticing. She pushed her hands down to her side as he stood, towering over her. There in the sunlight with bumblebees prowling over the fragrant clover field and his brothers watching, time seemed to stand still. All she could hear was the racing of her heart; all she could see was Tyrell's dark, dark eyes warm upon her as he lifted a curl from her cheek with his fingertip.

She couldn't ignore the brief kiss that brushed her lips. She wished her lips didn't answer his. She wished she hadn't blushed down to her boots. "You're in trouble," she managed huskily.

He lifted an eyebrow. "I know. Big trouble. Would you go to dinner with me tonight? There's a potluck and dance at the community hall, a small town thing, just before the Fourth of July's big rodeo and race. If you're not afraid, that is."

"Afraid of what?" She'd been terrified in her lifetime, but she'd never felt more safe than in Jasmine.

"Of me. Of you. Of us," he answered too quietly. "I'd like to hold you in my arms while we dance. I'd like to walk you home later and give you a good-night kiss under the moon."

The romantic image of Tyrell walking beside her through the night and drawing her into his arms terrified her. She shivered as he took her hand and carefully eased his fingers through hers, a contrast of light and dark, male and female. His dark sultry look said he wanted her now.

She swallowed and tried to remember why she'd hunted him down, why she wasn't running away. "The washer and dryer. I can't keep it."

"It's for me," he said gently, smoothing his other hand over her hair and toying with it. "I'll buy the laundry supplies if you do my wash. Or you can deduct your use of them from my rent and I'll do the laundry. Deal?"

"Well, the tub then," she argued, trying to hold her ground. "I can't keep that lovely old thing."

"If I'm going to look civilized and ready for the financial world, I'm going to need that, too."

Her knees were going weak at that dark hungry look, the erotic movements of his fingers in her hair. She knew in another minute that she'd be moving against his touch like a kitten being petted; the image didn't fit, not with her. "I guess it would be a savings. But I do not know if you are civilized," she said very carefully.

"You get to me." Tyrell's tone wasn't brooding, it was spoken more like an honest truth.

"Why? Because I'm out to prove—"

His finger on her lips stopped her. "It's that old man-woman thing. You excite me, honey."

She found herself smiling up at him, feeling soft and warm and feminine.

"Hey, Celine. Are you going to kill him now, or after supper?" Rio asked as she drew her hand from Tyrell's and backed a step away.

"Get lost, Rio," Tyrell ordered in a too pleasant tone as he placed his arm around Celine and drew her close to his side.

The protective and natural gesture startled her and for a heartbeat, while her knees were still weak, she leaned into the security of his warmth and strength. Then she pushed free, because his gentleness terrified her more than his hunger.

"You're just making my life difficult, Blaylock. You can't reach out and touch my hair and kiss me in front of everyone. I'm killing you," Celine restated firmly. She ignored the brothers who were grinning and studying the scene.

"Oh, how?" Tyrell's grin caused her flush to deepen and he bent to nuzzle and nip the other side of her throat.

This time, she was certain her shiver shook the earth. She hauled and scraped all the pieces of her body and mind back together. "Stop nibbling me. You said you were…considering marrying me. You actually told Neil Morris and Channing that. They came to ask me if it was true. I didn't have much time to talk with them because I had to find you. I hiked all the way up to your cabin and you weren't there. You weren't anywhere. For some reason I didn't expect you to be here, but I thought

I'd ask anyway. You seem to like to hold yourself apart and brood a lot. A man who broods is not a happy man.''

''I seem to remember something said last night about the subject of marriage. My parents had a happy one and so does the rest of my family.... You've found me. Now what are you going to do to me?'' he asked with interest, and with his back to his brothers, Tyrell's gaze lowered to her breasts. She tried not to breathe, because each breath pushed her nipples against the thin cloth. She tried to force the memory of his tormenting mouth into the dirt and couldn't.

''We can take care of him if you like,'' James offered and handed Tyrell a bouquet of wild daisies that the brothers had quickly picked. ''We haven't punched him around for a good long time.''

Apparently unthreatened by his brothers, Tyrell solemnly held out the daisies to her, hooked his thumbs into his jeans and waited.

''No, thanks. I like to take care of my own problems. Thank you, but I am not Hillary-poo,'' she said before grabbing the bouquet and shooting a fist into Tyrell's stomach. Clutching the flowers, she walked back to her truck.

Tyrell rubbed his stomach, admired the solid punch and ignored his brothers' guffaws. He was too busy watching the fast sway of Celine's bottom and thinking of how that softness had felt in his hands.

''You're drooling, boy,'' Logan said when he found breath to talk, his tone filled with laughter.

''Huh?'' Tyrell asked, noting the soft shimmering flow of Celine's breasts as she turned to glare at him.

''Try roses next time,'' Roman offered as he wiped away the tears his laughter had caused.

''Huh? Oh, I did. That's what she's mad about.''

''Try doing the laundry and cooking supper,'' James, an experienced husband, offered.

''I did that, too, and I asked her for a date. She's cute, isn't she? I mean the way she gets all huffy and scowls at me. She seems to glitter with those frothy curls and those green eyes.''

"Man, you're a sorry excuse for a Blaylock," Dan said with a grin. He punched Tyrell on the shoulder, a brotherly gesture. "You've been in the mountains too long. You can't even get a date with the woman you're mooning over. You'll ruin our reputation, prior to married life, of course.''

Celine hauled out her tire jack, hefted another bald tire from the back of her pickup and Tyrell walked to her. "I'll do that.''

"Leave me alone. I can take care of myself.''

"Sure you can. Try that on Channing and Neil, not me,'' he said, tugging the rusty old jack away from her, though she resisted. "You need a new jack, new tires and a new pickup wouldn't hurt, either,'' he said and began to change the tire.

Celine crouched beside him. "Checking your work, city boy,'' she snapped.

Tyrell realized that he was flexing his muscles to impress her, no better than a teenager showing off for his girl. Sunlight danced through her hair and her freckles showed clearly, enticing him, but her eyes were all green fire, lashing at him. "Take it easy, Celine. In another minute, you're going to explode.''

"You're asking for it, Blaylock.''

Tyrell couldn't resist a grin or teasing her. "Be nice, Lomax. You know you love me. What about that dinner and dance tonight?''

Celine glared at him. "I've got a big headache that is getting bigger just thinking about it. The answer is no.''

After she burned a dusty trail away from him, Tyrell turned to his brothers and studied them. Celine's visit had made him feel almost like a boy with his first girl; she made him feel clean and alive and ready to start life. "What was that about punching me around?'' he asked before spreading his arms and leaping upon his brothers.

* * *

Early on that hot July Saturday night, Celine studied Channing and Neil over her poker hand at Mamie's Café. Clearly they'd forgotten about charming her after Tyrell had given them the impression that she was his. So much for her power to draw men like flies. They'd accepted her as men usually did as "one of the boys," and she was comfortable with that role. With Channing's shirt unbuttoned at the throat, his tie awry and a growth of beard on his smoothly tanned cheeks, he almost looked like a working man. Across the table littered with toothpicks for bids, potato chips and iced colas, Neil Morris was worrying if she had that last ace—Celine played her hand, placing the cards faceup on the table. "Read 'em and weep, gentlemen."

"Stud poker used to be my game," Neil's tone mourned a time when he was king and all was right with the land.

She scraped the toothpicks toward her as Channing and Neil groaned. Long isolated stretches in blizzard conditions had honed the poker skills she'd learned from Cutter and Link—without the cheating methods. She frowned at the couples dancing on the floor to the old slow dancing songs. Tyrell had held her gently like that. "There's a dinner and dance tonight," she said, hoping to start a conversation about the intricacies of dating.

"Deal," Channing ordered, intent upon retrieving his lost bets.

Tyrell disturbed her. She kept seeing him riding toward her, standing in front of her, a boyish grin pasted on his face, and all those muscles and cords covered by tanned gleaming skin.

Relaxed, she studied Channing and Neil, who were both sizing up the woman who had just walked in. They turned back to the table when a big man wearing a wedding ring and carrying a baby entered and looped his arm around her. Channing and Neil sighed, a chorus of forlorn males.

Celine propped her boots up on the extra chair. She was tired from tramping up Tyrell's mountain, and she couldn't rest, nei-

tled by her confrontation with him earlier. All dark skin gleaming with sweat and muscles sliding beneath it, Tyrell's body was mouthwatering. She'd wanted to reach out and place her hand on that bulge of muscle on his upper arm. She'd wanted to skim her palm down his chest, over his flat stomach and— The laughter in his eyes had caused her stomach to tighten almost painfully.

She was at ease with Neil and Channing and had listened to their comments about women in the café. "Pass," was Channing's comment. "Yours," Neil had said dully when women did not appeal to him.

"So what is that growling, getting-hot thing men do?" the woman who was one of the boys asked her comfortable companions.

Channing choked on his sip of iced tea. Neil crushed the potato chips in his hands. They crumbled to the table as both men stared blankly at her. Channing placed his glass on the table—almost. It toppled to the floor and crashed.

"What?" Celine asked, wondering what had disturbed her friends. She arranged the cards Channing had dealt. "It's sort of a punctuation after a really intense kiss."

Channing and Neil looked at each other. Neil grinned. "Tyrell?"

Celine picked up her cards and arranged them. "I just don't get it.... Bid," she said, tossing toothpicks onto the center of the table.

"This is far more interesting than poker, darling," Channing purred, placing his cards facedown on the table.

"I think Tyrell may be sensitive. I think I hurt his feelings. He asked me for a date," she said, curious to see what the men would say about Tyrell asking her for a date. "I'm not the dating kind. He knows that. I've never had time to play games."

"I've known Tyrell all my life. He has never been sensitive. Well, maybe if he didn't place first at a math event in high school. Then he'd brood a bit.... He's a dog, asking you for a date. Is that the way a man should act when he wants to herd a girl to the altar? He has no shame," Neil purred with a grin.

Channing looked past Celine's shoulder and murmured dryly, "Growler alert."

The hair on Celine's nape lifted as Tyrell eased his tall body into a chair. She fought the warm leap of her blood as she noted he'd just come from a shower, his hair still damp, and his delicious scent mixed with that of soap. The dress shirt was customary Western male dress, rolled up at the forearms, neatly tucked into worn, pressed jeans. His boots weren't the worn Western ones of today, but brightly polished. Clearly Tyrell was ready for a small town Saturday night. He looked delicious. "Gentlemen...Celine," he murmured coolly as the other men grinned at him. "Am I interrupting?"

"I said everything I wanted to this afternoon," she said firmly. "Go away."

Channing recovered quickly. "Miss Lomax was just telling us that you growl after a really good kiss."

"Then there's that getting-hot thing," Neil added, clearly suppressing a grin. "Why would you do such a thing, Tyrell?"

Celine flushed as Tyrell slowly, thoroughly studied her. Tiny little lightning bolts zipped through the air between them. Celine discovered her hand slowly moving upward to smooth his cheek—he looked as if he needed petting, like a wary stray who needed a home.

Channing cleared his throat. "I suppose you have plans to attend the big rodeo and race tomorrow, Celine."

She jerked back the hand that was midway to Tyrell's smoothly shaven face. "Got a big day tomorrow up on the mountain. Got that Blaylock job to do. It's going to take a long, long time and put a lot of money in my account. Have to go," she said, preparing to rise and make her escape. "See you guys around."

Another thought terrified her. She looked at Tyrell and imagined him, torn and bloody, on the horns of a bull. "You're not going to be in that rodeo, are you?"

"I feel like I'd like to tangle with something big and mean now," he said.

She reached out to touch his shoulder. "Don't, ah, you're probably out of shape and—" When Tyrell leveled a dark stare at her, the vein in his temple pulsing heavily, she decided to escape. "Bye."

All three men stood, towering over her. Tyrell drew her chair away and brought her free hand to his mouth. The dark meaning in his eyes terrified and shot liquid heat through her at the same time. His kiss burned her palm as she carried it out into the moonlit night in her tight fist.

An hour later at seven o'clock, she decided to pot the plants that Else had dropped by. The brilliant salmon-colored impatiens would be perfect in the shadows of the old gas station and lined on the concrete blocks once used for pumps. While she was hunting for Tyrell, she'd found an old wooden chair along the road, and had tossed it into her pickup. A few blows from her hammer as she thought about Tyrell's courtly marriage statement, and the chair was sturdy again, perfect to place in the front of her office. She felt like puttering, a restless need that came upon her when her eyes and body were tired. She didn't understand her impulse to touch Tyrell Blaylock, but she would bury it with the plants.

She went outside, emptied her wagon and took a shovel to the back, where a garden once grew. She scanned the old poles used to stake beans and tomatoes, the little picket fence in shambles that had once protected the garden, then sank her shovel into the dark, rich earth. When her wagon was filled, she topped it with discarded empty clay pots piled against the building and pulled it around to the front of the gas station.

"You!" She stared at Tyrell, who was sitting on the chair and had tipped it back against the station's rock wall. His arms were crossed over his chest and his stare wasn't friendly; it ripped down her body and jarred her.

"You're giving me a complex," he said darkly, studying her. "And you're afraid and running from me. I'm not like your father and I'm not like Cutter. I have never hurt a woman in my lifetime. I never will."

"Me, afraid and running? Not on your life. *But you are,*" she shot back, because she knew how to defend herself—she'd had years of practice.

He tilted his head, the dying sunlight gleaming on his black hair; his eyes narrowed. "How so?"

"You're brooding over something that has nothing to do with the land I'm taking away from you. It's written all over you. You can't wait to get back to your hideout. All that business about a date was just stuff men toss around. You were showing off for your brothers and I won't be paying for your problems."

"Lomax, you've got a real narrow opinion of men, don't you?"

She didn't answer; she didn't want to think of Cutter or Link just now, or her revenge on the Blaylocks. She crouched to fill the pots, furiously stuffing the tender plants into them.

"Jeans would be okay for the dance. You've got a good pair and a nice cotton blouse—I washed and ironed them both. The food is good. Home cooking," Tyrell stated lazily behind her. "We wouldn't have to go together. I'll meet you there, that way it won't seem like the date you're so afraid of."

"Nobody irons clothes anymore," Celine muttered. "And I'm not afraid of a date with you. It's just not going to happen, that's all."

"I say you are afraid," he teased with a grin that devastated her. "Of actually going on a date with me, riding in my car with me to a dinner and dance."

Six

Celine stiffened as Tyrell placed his hand low on her back and opened the door to Jasmine's community hall. She tensed, resisting the wide, warm span of his hand guiding her inside. It wasn't a pushy shove, or rough, or sensuous, but rather a gentle touch. She wasn't used to men opening doors for her, though she'd seen the courtesy shown to other women. "I can find my own way, Blaylock. You don't have to guide me."

Tyrell smiled slowly, humor softening his face. "It's a man-woman kind of thing, Lomax. Dad treated Mother with courtesy and respect, and taught us to treat women the same." He reached down to hook a finger in the back of her jeans and tug lightly. "Do you have a problem with family traditions?"

"Well, it's okay…I guess. When in Rome and all that." She couldn't argue with the respect that Tyrell paid his mother, or his family traditions. She had one family tradition—revenge. She sucked in air and entered the room dominated by Blaylocks. Here she was, a Lomax, right in the heart of the Blaylocks. Easily identified by their height and rangy build, the Blaylocks reflected their Native American and conquistador heritage. With children hitched on their hips, wives and husbands tugged against them, they were definitely a family who stayed close, just as Cutter had said. Other families blended with them and the sound of children laughing, gossip and excitement hurled toward Celine, enveloping her.

Tyrell gave her a little push forward, then took her hand in his as the entire crowd looked at them and silence filled the room. She hadn't held hands in her lifetime and Tyrell's big warm one seemed like a lifeline now. She realized how they must have looked, Tyrell standing slightly behind her, almost as if he had posed her with him to make a statement. "What's wrong? Why are they looking at us?" she whispered.

"Not a thing. Everything is just right."

"Did you bring her—Hillary—here?" Celine knew she did not match the streamlined elegance of Hillary. She tried to ease a distance away from Tyrell, tugging at her hand, so that people wouldn't think—

"No, just you." The answer was curt and suddenly all the tall dark Blaylock men whooped as Dan kissed his red-haired wife, Hannah. Each man tugged his respective mate into his arms and kissed her thoroughly.

"I was hoping that wouldn't happen until you'd relaxed a bit. Sorry, but it's a Blaylock tradition," Tyrell muttered, before he tugged her close against him.

Held tight against his taut hard body, Celine was bent back over his arm as his mouth slanted hungrily upon hers. She grabbed his shoulders to secure herself against a tropical storm of color and dark, mysterious, exciting tastes. The kiss softened and beckoned and curled warmly around her. His teeth nibbled lightly at her bottom lip and his mouth changed, slanted more intimately as his big hands opened on her back. He drew her closer until she stood on tiptoe.

Tyrell's mouth eased to brush against her and all she could

hear was her blood rushing through her veins. He looked down at her in that dark hungry way and her breath flew away from her and she shot out a hand, anchoring to a chair as her knees began to give way.

Tyrell's smile grew as he bent to kiss her briefly once more. "I wouldn't have done that, but it is a family tradition."

"Is it going to happen again?" she asked shakily just as Rio grabbed Paloma and led her into a fancy dance step. Then he bent her over his arm and kissed her.

"Sorry," Tyrell said with a grin that said he wasn't sorry at all, and dived in for another mind-blowing, hungry kiss. This time, he framed her face with his hands. When the kiss was over, she realized she'd locked her arms tightly around his waist, seeking more of the delight and mystery that was Tyrell.

Those dark, dark eyes filled with her and she followed her instincts to lightly nip at his bottom lip. Tyrell's hands tightened and his entire body tensed. His breathing shook the air around her and he seemed to flinch as if taking a blow.

She couldn't resist lightly brushing her lips over his, just that once, and the room seemed to drift away as Tyrell's hard face gentled and he smoothed the curls back from her cheek. She didn't know how much time passed as his thumb smoothed her temple and they stood looking at each other.

A last call to dinner jolted Celine. She tore herself away, shaking and flushing with embarrassment. Tyrell looped his arm around her and drew her to his side as he talked with his family and neighbors and then they were sitting, side by side at a picnic table covered by a red-checkered oilcloth. Unused to being held, Celine sat very stiffly; the novelty of being smaller, feminine and courted terrified her. Her elbow in his ribs went unnoticed. Tyrell suddenly stopped talking to Roman and turned to look down at her. The look held and warmed and Celine trembled at the impact. He took her hand and held it in his on his jeaned thigh as if they'd always come here, as if they were meant to be together.

Celine watched the Blaylocks very carefully. Each male attended his wife with a long meaningful look, a slow caress—

She stiffened, noting that James's hand was slowly caressing his wife's back. It wasn't a sensuous caress, rather a soothing, pleasant one—Celine knew, because Tyrell's large hand was slowly warming her back, up and down, across her shoulders, and his touch did not seem at all improper. She'd been arching luxuriously to his touch. "Hey!" she whispered desperately to him, sharply nudging him with her elbow. "Stop it. You're cuddling me."

"So?" Clearly Tyrell wasn't bothered by his display of affection for her.

"Why?" she said, floundering in this strange new fascinating world.

"It's that old man-woman thing I guess. Seems natural with you."

"You know, of course, that I'm usually considered to be one of the boys, not cuddling material. You've had a hard few months, losing your job and all. You could be off balance."

"Uh-uh. You feel too soft and curvy and warm to be one of the boys." But his hand didn't stop caressing until his arm reached around her for a brief hug. After his arm slid away, Celine sat very still, stunned by the easy affection.

When the tables were cleared, a toddler came to sit on her lap, pushing his finger through one of her curls. He giggled in delight. "Pretty. Pretty lady."

"Aren't you a charmer?" she cooed, delighted by the cuddly baby, and found Tyrell watching her again.

"I'd like a family. Would you?" he asked quietly as the toddler slid from her lap.

"I don't know if I have the ability to be a mother. My mother left me when I was a year old. She didn't like the mess or the trouble and they said she couldn't love me because I'd hurt her so in childbirth. I could be like her. But sometimes I see what other people have," she answered honestly, "and I

wonder how it would feel to have all that warmth around me."
She watched a mother rock her daughter's doll and pain tore
at Celine again. She hadn't been allowed dolls; Cutter had demanded that she play with traditional boys' toys—dump trucks
and cowboy guns and race cars.

Tyrell scanned the hall filled with people he'd known for a
lifetime. "Good," he said simply. "It was a really good way
to grow up and to live. I should have stayed or at least come
back more often."

She caught that swift dark pain in his expression and then it
was gone. What clung to Tyrell, hurting him? "You'll work it
out," she said, meaning it. "You're a thorough man. You'll
find the answer."

His gaze skimmed over her, warming her face. "I know.
You do look pretty tonight, 'pretty lady.'"

She swallowed the sharp defensive rebuff that sprang to her
lips, and looked away. In her lifetime, no man had seen her as
pretty. She couldn't trust the joyous feelings within her. Could
she?

"You look okay, yourself," she returned unevenly, fearing
to look at him as he laughed outright. Tyrell looked more than
okay; he looked delicious.

The tiny band began to play and Roman gave Kipp to Tyrell.
"Change him. I'm dancing with my wife."

Tyrell actually winced at the toddler who looked like an
angel and smelled quite different. Tyrell's expression was a
mix of frustration, disgust and a plea for help as he looked at
Celine. "I don't suppose—"

"I'm out of here," she said, laughing at the way he held
Kipp at arm's length.

Later, Tyrell found her in a quiet corner, sipping iced tea
and studying the close-knit community. She picked the laughter
and warmth apart to find Cutter's lying, treacherous gang. She
couldn't; she found friends and couples and children who
would grow up protected and safe and free. People who had

been friends for years were excited about the rodeo and race. She found mothers who cuddled sleepy little ones, and who, with a laugh, nudged husbands into dancing. There were eighty-year-old cowboys with slicked and neatly parted hair dancing with girls and elderly women alike. The Blaylock men placed their hands on their wives' backs, guiding them, just as Tyrell had done. They teased their wives, but gently, and love flowed between them. Each wife acted as if she knew she was respected and enjoyed the courtship that continued even after marriage. A touch to her husband's raven hair didn't go unnoticed; each Blaylock male responded instantly with a dark slow look that spoke of love. Else's husband clearly cherished her as his lady love. Threaded with laughter, love flowed around the room like magic.

Cutter's bitter words slashed at Celine, ''Never trust a Blaylock. They'll get you. It's all for show, how they treat their women, but a man isn't sweet like that behind the bedroom doors, you can believe that.''

Logan Blaylock passed her, a sleepy toddler draped across his broad shoulder. How could each child look as if he were loved and cherished if he wasn't? Children knew with perfect clarity how adults felt toward them—she'd known how Cutter resented her not being a boy. She'd known that he'd resented any small expenses. As a child she'd scrunched herself into a shadowy tiny ball, but these children were vibrant and free and happy. She watched Else help an elderly man onto the dance floor and chat with him as they barely moved in the dance. James looped his arm around his wife's arm as she came to stand beside him. Dan kissed Hannah's hand before tucking it within his.

Tyrell had grown up like this and now he made his way toward her, easing the sleeping baby in his arms to Else as he passed. His eyes never left her, as if he'd come for her for years to come and nothing could keep him away.

"Come here, my lady." The words were tender and rich and dark, floating upon her, around her.

My lady. He meant her! The term was courtly and delightful, curled within her like a treasure. She shivered, fearing the pleasure, the softness as he took her hand to draw her onto the dance floor. When he put her hand on his shoulder and placed his hand on her waist, it was as if he were fitting them for life. Then he took her free hand so slowly, and curled it in his, bringing it to rest upon his chest, just there, over his heart. Tyrell held her in a lovely, old-fashioned gallant way as they moved around the room. Other dancers moved aside as Tyrell guided her through a lovely old waltz.

Along the side, the Blaylocks stood, husbands and wives and children held close, smiling as Tyrell danced Celine slowly around the room. It was just one dance, a waltz, and she would remember it for the rest of her life.

When the music ended, Tyrell kept moving with her and she wished the night would never stop. Every look and touch made her feel uniquely feminine and treasured. With a lifetime of missed proms and dances behind her, she would cherish this dreamy evening forever.

Then James kissed his wife and Joe grabbed Else, and with a whoop the other brothers tugged their wives close for searing kisses.

"Sorry," Tyrell murmured before he slowly bent to fit his lips to hers.

She laughed then, not alone anymore, and reached her arms up to hold him close.

When the kiss was done and Tyrell was looking steamy and pleased with himself, Celine couldn't resist. "Sorry," she said and reached for his face, bringing him down for her brief kiss.

Immediately the Blaylocks set off another round of spouse kissing and Tyrell jerked back, staring down at her as if he was shaken by the surprise. He shuddered, his hands locking onto her waist, smoothing the indenture and lowering briefly to her hips, jerking her body to his. His jaw tightened, his expression hardening. She wasn't afraid of him, or that glimpse of something hot and primitive that ran beneath Tyrell's smooth veneer before he controlled the emotion.

Later, at her doorstep, he bent to kiss the side of her cheek, and groaned heavily as she lifted her mouth to his. "It's been a long day," he said unevenly as he stared down at her, his hands tightening on her arms.

"That family tradition," Celine began as she studied his mouth and thought of his taste, desperate and hungry, upon her lips. "Just how many women have you kissed like that, all night long."

"Not a one since I was seventeen and showing off." The answer slid softly, powerfully at her, pushing her breath away from her keeping.

She ran a trembling hand through her hair and tried not to shiver. "That was a few years ago."

"A lot of years, honey," he agreed softly and slid his finger through a curl and toyed with it. "I'm not all that experienced, either."

Stunned, she grabbed his shirt. "Tyrell Blaylock, don't you tease me. I won't have it."

"But you respond so perfectly." Tyrell studied her upturned face and ran his thumb across her bottom lip. Then he groaned again and walked to his four-wheeler; it purred away, taking her good-night kiss with it. Celine rubbed her trembling hands over her hot face. She'd wanted one of those long, sweet, slow kisses, and she supposed Tyrell had what he wanted—showing the Blaylocks that he could get a Lomax woman to respond to him.

After a sleepless night, she wasn't in the mood for Tyrell leaning over her at dawn. "I thought you were cheery in the morning," he said and ran a daisy under her nose. "Or is that just when someone else wants to sleep?"

She'd gathered the precious bouquet to her sometime at night and the flowers lay crushed around and beneath her. She blew at the daisy brushing her nose and stealthily drew up the quilt to hide the smashed bouquet. She turned on her stomach. "Go away, Blaylock. See you when the rent is due. Better yet—mail it. I've got a hard day's work ahead of me."

"Up!" He patted her bottom, stunning her. She turned to hit him with a pillow and pulled the quilt over her head; it didn't muffle his chuckle.

She flipped to her back and stared up at him. Dressed in a white T-shirt and worn jeans, Tyrell was freshly shaved and showered.

"You're going to the rodeo. Fine. Die in a pool of blood. Let me sleep."

"I've got something else in mind, though I'd like a try at Logan's bucking bull."

She shot out a hand, fearing for him. "You wouldn't…would you? It's just macho, show-off stuff, and you could get hurt."

"You're prettier, but if I can't have you, I would purely like to ride that bull."

She blew away the curl that was bobbing onto her nose. "Let me get this straight, Blaylock. This is some sort of blackmail, right? You'd go to that rodeo, get hurt and it would be my fault, right? How typical."

His grin dazzled her. He looked gorgeous; she felt rumpled, grumpy, drained and caught with daisy-evidence smashed beneath her. She flopped over onto her stomach again and flipped back after Tyrell swatted her bottom. "Hey! Lay off."

He stood there, grinning down at her, black hair gleaming in the dim light and she remembered how he had left her at her doorstep; she'd wanted that dreamy good-night kiss and the hunger she'd tasted on his lips. "You got what you wanted last night, didn't you?" she shot at him.

"Not exactly," he answered with a chuckle that ignited her temper.

She launched herself up out of the bed and straight at him. Surprised, Tyrell wrapped his arms around her as the movement propelled him backward. Reacting, he swept her up in his arms, carried her back to the bed and tossed her in it. With a laugh, he followed, pinning her down with his body.

The bed creaked beneath them as Celine struggled to free her wrists from his hands. Breathing hard, she held very still as Tyrell's expression slid from pleasure to a darker emotion, and his gaze slid down her bare legs, tangled with his jeaned ones. He looked slowly up the length of her body and inhaled sharply as he looked down at the T-shirt covering her breasts.

He kissed her then, desperately, as if he'd torn free of his leashes, his mouth fiery and demanding. Celine leaped into the passion, burning with it, and Tyrell's big hands went to her breasts. She tensed, aching, uncertain, watching him above her, his expression harsh and desperate. She wanted to soothe him, wanted to lift her hand and smooth back that black spear of hair crossing his forehead. She traced his eyebrows and knew that something shifted within Tyrell at her touch. He waited, very still as she experimentally ran a fingertip over his other brow. It was almost as if her touch tethered him, held him from shadows she did not understand. The idea that her touch could affect him fascinated her.

Suddenly he tore free to sit up on the bed, his back to her, his hands in his face, his muscles tense. "No," he said too quietly, unevenly. "I didn't come for this."

Unable to resist, she placed her hand on his back and the hard muscles there rippled and tensed at her touch.

"No, don't touch me." His deep voice was desperately ragged as if he were fighting a war within himself.

She had to touch him, or she'd shatter. She ran her hand slowly up and down his back, just as he had done the night before. The stroke served to bring herself back into one piece, tethering him to her for a precious bit of time. "Yes, like that," he whispered less shakily.

A horse nickered outside and Tyrell turned to look at her over his shoulder, surveying her flushed face and trembling body amid the rumpled pillows. "We've got a problem, Lomax. You are a passionate and feminine woman. I don't want what we have to be any more tangled than it is. There is a logical order to this, and bypassing the traditional stops ruins that order. Would you consider spending the day with me? I raided Else's refrigerator and we can ride up on the mountain."

A tiny thrill circled Celine as they stared at each other, and she forced herself to breathe. "Is this another date?"

"Uh-huh. The first wasn't so bad, was it?" He looked wary and uncertain and alone. He was a logical man dealing with emotions that clearly haunted him. He'd come to her when he could have gone elsewhere; he'd preferred her to anyone else. The heady thought caused her to smile. She could spare a day to know more about Tyrell's shadows.

"Sure," she said lightly as she looked at Tyrell's hand around hers. "A free dinner is a free dinner."

"Thanks. You do wonders for my ego and stop smirking. That dimple sets me off."

She fluttered her lashes playfully at him because she felt young and feminine and fascinating. It was her first attempt at lash-fluttering, but at the moment, she just had to try.

Tyrell grinned. "Lay off," he said and pushed her face gently with his open hand until she lay back on the pillow. "I'll wait outside."

He'd wanted to bring her here, away from the gas station that still held bullets from Cutter's shootout with Luke Blaylock. He didn't want to share her at the rodeo; he'd wanted her alone, sharing a part of his life that few had entered. After riding a portion of the original Blaylock homestead, Tyrell brought her to his favorite place. The tiny waterfall poured from the black rocks into a small, crystal clear lake. After the picnic lunch, Celine tramped around the meadow, looking for the boundary rocks, while Tyrell lay back on the blanket, enjoying the day with Celine. "Find any trace of the boundary markers you think exist?" he asked when she returned to stand over him.

He tilted his head to one side, just a bit, to take in the curve of her breasts, enjoying the view.

"No, but I will and the big house that Cutter said he'd built." She took off her ball cap and ran her fingers through her hair. Above Tyrell, dressed in a battered T-shirt and cutoff jeans and work boots, she was curved, womanly and he heard himself groan.

"You should see a doctor. You sound like you're coming down with something. It wouldn't be any fun to ruin you, if you're sick," she said, as Tyrell launched himself to his feet. Her green eyes widened as he wrapped his arms around her, gently imprisoning her.

"I don't want you hitting me when I tell you this."

"If it's about my grandfather, I know what you're going to say. Okay, I'll listen. Why did you bring me here? What do you want to say? I'm not taking bribes and I know when a man has to set his own time and place—I've worked with enough of them. Of course, you're showing off that you're bigger and stronger than I am, that typical male power thing, but I'm—"

His light kiss stopped her. "Your revenge has nothing to do with this. I want you to listen, Lomax, very carefully."

She blew a curl from her face. "What?"

Tyrell wanted to laugh, but he knew that Celine's temper would ignite and then what he wanted to say would have to wait. "I find you very attractive." *Attractive?* He mocked himself. He looked at her and he knew how she'd respond, delighted in the fire within her.

"Uh-huh..." she murmured warily, sunlight dancing off her lashes, the freckles crossing her nose seemed like bits of magic.

"Exciting. Womanly. You're the most feminine woman I know. If I would have really kissed you last night, I would have wanted more. I would have wanted to wake up in your bed, tangled with you and I'd have more than likely been in you. Because that's where I want to be now. But that isn't what I want for the long term. Making love to you would complicate—it is complicating—" he corrected. "I want a relationship with you. I want to give you flowers and take you to dances and picnics and more than that. I want to cherish you, Celine. I already do."

Her fine red-gold eyebrows drew together in a scowl, not a receptive expression. Tyrell released her. He'd given her notice; he wanted Celine to see him coming for her and know what he wanted. He wanted no mistakes about his intentions. "Think about it, sweetheart."

She stiffened and turned to walk away from him. Then she turned back. "You want something."

He had to laugh at that. "Oh, I truly do."

"Men don't find me feminine, Tyrell. I've always been one of the boys. This has to do with why I'm here."

"I'm glad you're here." He couldn't resist trailing a finger across her lips and watching her eyes darken to meadow-green. "Just think about it, okay?"

"Me? 'Feminine'? That's what you said last night, too."

"Every succulent bit of you. You drive me crazy when you eat, slowly, sucking on your fingers and that little tongue— It's not just that. You fascinate me. Right down to that dimple when you smirk."

"All that fascination stops after sex, Blaylock. The game ends."

"Oh, really? Tell me more," he invited, once again fascinated by the woman he had waited for all his lifetime.

She blushed and looked away, and Tyrell had to shove his

hands into his back pockets to keep from reaching for her. "It hurt," she whispered and he ached for what she had missed.

She turned to him suddenly. "Why? Why me?"

"Instincts. I've always had good ones, and you make me happy. I haven't been happy in a long time, honey." He took her hand and placed it on the back of his neck, the sleek strands warmed beneath her touch as did the hard, tense muscles of his body. She smoothed them with her fingertips, and something within Tyrell seemed to ease. He waited patiently as she experimented, smoothing her fingertips across his cheek. In a gesture so tender it terrified her, Tyrell turned his head to rest against her palm. She felt as if it were a coming home, as if he belonged to her, and she belonged to him.

She jerked her hand back, terrified by the new knowledge that she had so much power over this strong man. "Oh, my," she whispered, shaken.

"Yes, 'oh, my,'" Tyrell agreed in a deep, raw tone as he drew her glasses from her and carefully placed them on the thermal picnic basket.

"You're going to kiss me, aren't you," she stated, knowing he was and she would kiss him back.

"I have to. Be gentle with me, honey."

"What's going on here, Tyrell?" she asked shakily.

"You'll find out," he returned easily, already drawing her into his arms.

The second week of July, Tyrell punched numbers into his calculator and then fed them into the computer on his desk. The enchiladas just needed popping into the oven, the lettuce and fresh tomatoes already chopped and waiting, the cheese grated. He liked taking care of Celine, of being "home" when she returned from the courthouse searching for records. He enjoyed what he was doing—helping build lives instead of corporate profits. His clients were now couples saving for homes, parents preparing for their children's college education and elderly people securing their investments. He glanced up to see Celine studying him as she passed, her expression wary. Since they'd spent that Sunday on the mountain, he had been the subject of her curious glances. Celine was definitely studying him, her feminine curiosity an excitement in itself. He realized he'd just caught her scent, mixed with musty paper and oil from her pickup. He wanted to give her time to think about him, to trust him. To adjust to the relationship between a Blaylock and a Lomax. If he snapped his leashes and she responded, he was lost. He wanted more. Much more. He wanted to marry Celine. While he wanted to call her "sweetheart," he knew she wouldn't appreciate the endearment, not now. "Celine."

"Blaylock. You know I'm taking my time with this project, don't you? That the bill is going to be quite hefty."

"I'd like to make an advance payment on that, if it suits you," he said, knowing that she needed money. "You can add a nonrefundable clause to the contract, if you want."

Taking money from him wasn't easy for her, but in the end, because she was a practical woman, she did.

Tyrell studied her soft bottom as she hurried back into the garage and his mouth went dry. He ached to take her, to make love to her. Working in the same room with her tested his willpower. He wanted her to know him, to give her time. For that reason, he had carefully reined himself. Ordinarily he didn't have a problem with control. But Celine's green eyes and freckles and curvy body and— He groaned again and turned back to his work, burying himself in it. Patience and cool methods had always served him well, and now, in the pursuit of Celine, they were destroying him bit by bit. He heard the bath water running and groaned again. He stood, and after running his hands down his jaw and through his hair, he looked into the small mirror she'd rummaged from a thrift shop and saw a frustrated man.

If he traveled up and down from the mountain each day, a little of his body's need for Celine might be trimmed away.

He doubted anything would diminish his need for her, to feel her touch, to see those wide green eyes delighted with the daisy bouquet he'd picked for her. With mountain daisies dotting her red-gold curls, she had looked like a bride.

The mirror reflected a desperate man, one with sleepless nights behind and ahead of him. Tyrell stopped the groan moving up his throat.

For the next week, Celine attempted to get information on the adjoining land and to talk with the landowners about any changes they might have noticed. By carefully stacking her research for the survey, she hoped to find Cutter's landmarks. Mid-July was a perfect time to survey in the wild and soon she would begin—

She prowled through every moment of what Tyrell had told her on the mountain and how he felt, lying over her, shaking with a need that seemed to be torn from him. She liked the weight of him over her and her own needs had surprised her. She, a Lomax, liked to cuddle the tall Blaylock whose fierce storms seemed to ease within her arms.

She resented aching for him, for whatever pain he was walking through, trying to hold within himself.

From her desk in the office, Celine studied Tyrell as he counseled his elderly clients, mugs of morning coffee on his desk. Competent and friendly, he outlined which funds should be moved and why. He spoke in that deep, cool tone, unlike the man whose ragged whisper haunted her nights, "Celine…"

He punched buttons on his calculator, then fed the figures into his computer and turned the screen to the Monroes. They obviously trusted him, a Blaylock—a member of an honorable family long respected in the community.

But she was a Lomax and she had a duty to her grandfather. Her basic research was finished and she didn't want to think of how distracted she'd been when he'd come behind her, to slip his arms around her, just holding her in the fresh mountain air.

He'd tickled her, chasing her across a high mountain meadow. She'd never felt so light and carefree, but then she hadn't imagined that a grown man would like to play and tease.

She fingered the new gold studs in her earlobes—an unlikely whimsical purchase. Tyrell could kiss. And cuddle. She loved that slow caress of his hand on her back, and had found herself almost leaning into it. Then he had that slow sensuous nape-rubbing thing that melted her entire body. She tried to concentrate on the land abstracts in front of her and found herself listening to his recommendations to his clients. Tyrell's deep voice was certain, outlining the details of a better retirement plan. Sunlight from the windows lit the planes of his face, and Celine sniffed delicately, taking in his scent.

Her grandfather would have hated her, lashed at her for kissing Tyrell, for thinking of him, for dreaming of him. Tyrell's big hands moved quickly across the computer keys and desire tugged low in her body.

Could she trust him? This first man to want her, to make her feel very special and feminine and desired?

Tyrell's dark eyes flicked over her quickly and then he continued explaining the benefits of one financial program. That one glance staked her out and heated, claimed her and she found herself blushing. Tyrell glanced at her again and this time with humor, as if he knew her thoughts.

Celine shivered and pretended to study the paper in front of her. She had a mission to take back Lomax land; she couldn't let Tyrell Blaylock distract her.

The elderly Mr. Monroe looked at her, his expression wary. "You'd be Ms. Lomax?"

"Yes, I am."

"Tyrell says to trust you, and you can always trust a Blaylock. I remember your grandfather," he said quietly as if dark memories were skipping through him. "But I'd say that you'd be a horse of a different color…especially since Tyrell Blay-lock is so taken with you. Haven't known a Blaylock man yet to take up with a woman that wasn't special and true and good. You just come to the house when you want, Miss Goldilocks.''

"How well did you know my grandfather?'' she asked, wanting to know everything all at once. Perhaps if she couldn't find what she needed in the legal descriptions, she could find clues in the story of the people who knew Cutter.

The answer was curt. ''Well enough. I was one of the dep-uties who was with Luke Blaylock the night we had the shoot-out right here in this gas station. Cutter had just beaten up Monty Chevaz and—''

''Now, dear, that's enough,'' Mrs. Monroe murmured gently. ''The girl isn't like Cutter, not a bit. She's a sweet little thing. Wouldn't harm a fly, much less try to kill people. He did treat Garnet Blaylock very well, though.''

After the Monroes had left, Celine sat staring into space. ''My grandfather couldn't have lied,'' she finally said when the cold blood started moving in her body again.

She couldn't bear Tyrell's expression, those beautiful eyes dark with sympathy and concern. She rubbed her hands across her face. ''Something is very wrong here.''

''Celine, drop the whole thing. Make a life for yourself.'' Tyrell's hand was warm on her cold one. He drew her into the shelter of his arms. She could have rested there forever, pro-tected and safe, but she couldn't and tore herself away before the tears came.

He found her huddled in the kitchen, a dish towel soaking her tears. ''Oh, honey.''

Then he was angry, rage trembling in his deep voice. ''How many times have you been hurt? How many times have you hidden away crying like this?''

''Enough,'' she said truthfully, pushing past him.

He grabbed her arm and pulled her back against him. He tucked his chin over her head, holding her tight when she would have run away. "You're not alone any more, Celine. Try to trust me."

She wanted to mock him, to point out that she was a Lomax and he was a Blaylock and the two would mix like oil and water. She wanted to tear herself away. Instead she let him hold and rock her there in the soft light of the kitchen. "I never had a doll," she heard herself whimper distantly and hated her weakness as the painful past crept up on her.

Tyrell kept holding her and rocking in that gentle movement she found so strangely soothing, and Celine didn't know whether to be angry at him for getting under her shields or at herself for being so vulnerable. But at the same time, she wished he'd never let go.

Seven

Hours later Tyrell rose from his desk chair and studied Celine as she hurried across the street from the newspaper office. Pale and shaken, she clutched a yellow pad in her hand and her body leaned forward as though she'd been speared in her heart. She'd been in the newspaper office since she'd pulled herself together, and now, in the hot, dry mid-July sunlight, tears glittered on her face.

Tyrell wished he could spare Celine the pain she would uncover; he damned Cutter for his lies. She hurried around to the back of the garage and the Woodrows waited for Tyrell to return to their financial safety. "I'm sorry," he said. "This will have to wait."

"She's crying. She's a nice girl, even if she is the granddaughter to that scoundrel, Cutter. You'd better go to her," Mrs. Woodrow noted. "Come on, Herb. We've waited for forty years to retire and sell the farm and we can wait a day or so more. We need to go home and milk the cows anyway, Tyrell.

I did understand you correctly—that you would take a cow and calf in return for your services? To handle our account from now on?''

"You did," Tyrell answered, already moving toward the garage.

He found Celine in the evening shadows, looking small and helpless as she leaned against the old stone building. He reached out to smooth her curls away from her face and her tears seared his skin. "Celine...honey..."

"Go away." The sound was muffled, drenched in tears. She slashed at her face and Tyrell took away her glasses, which were awry. She grabbed them from his hand and tucked them in her shirt pocket as she looked away into the mountain shadows, avoiding him.

He reached out his hand to comfort and she swept it away. She seemed to crumple onto an old box, sitting with her head down, still clutching the pad. Tyrell crouched in front of her, and ached with each tear that dripped slowly from her clenched lids. "Celine?"

Her words seemed to be jerked painfully from her. "The old newspaper accounts tell about the shootout. They say Cutter was guilty of beating Monty Chevaz because he fired Cutter for stealing. Chevaz was in the hospital for weeks. In the local news, Cutter is listed in jail again and again."

Tyrell ran his hand through his hair. He was helpless to stop Celine in her journey to prove Cutter right. "I wish you could have been spared—"

"Everything is so easy for you, isn't it? All numbers lined up and everything oh-so logical. A family who loves you and worries about you. You know you're too talented to stay here, in this tiny town, and yet you're not leaving," she shot at him.

Tyrell sensed her need to argue, to wound. But he wasn't paying the price for Cutter's crimes. "I understand you're hurt," he began slowly.

Would she trust him? Would she let him hold her as he needed to do, to comfort her?

"You understand? *You understand?*" she demanded and jolted to her feet, her hands gesturing wildly. One slapped Tyrell's face with enough impact to jar him. He lifted his hand to rub his jaw and Celine frowned and reached to pat the injury gently. "Sorry. You've got to stay out of my way, Blaylock. I'm not happy now."

"I can see that."

"Well, it's my glasses. I need them. I can't tell how close you are without them," she said, hurrying to hide her pain. She took her glasses from her shirt pocket, shoved them on and crossed her arms in front of her, clutching the pad like a shield. "Cutter was framed, of course," she stated righteously.

Her tone challenged him. At thirty-four, she'd had years of believing lies and the truth was ugly enough without him underlining it. He admired her loyalty and he ached for her as the sordid details emerged. She squirmed from him as he lifted her glasses to wipe her eyes with his handkerchief. Tyrell reached out to cup the back of her head and placed the handkerchief over her nose. "Blow."

She complied and looked away from him. Then for a brief moment, she leaned her head against his chest and rested upon him. His arms were already folding her closer when she sniffed, lifted her head quickly and bumped him under the chin. With a sniff, she stepped back firmly and lifted her chin. "Sorry. Momentary relapse. I'm getting out of here."

She strode toward her pickup and nursed the engine into life and hurled off into the sunset. Tyrell stood very still and realized that she'd hurt him. He'd allowed few to penetrate his emotions, but Celine had dusted him away as though she'd never laughed in his arms, never lifted her lips to his. She reminded him of himself, keeping his pain too close and not wanting others to see. Was that what he'd done to his parents? Pushed them away when he feared he'd fail?

He was waiting for her when she came back later that night, her shoulders drooping. She closed the garage door and leaned tiredly against it. He wanted to hold her, to take away the pain. Instead he sat in the old rocker, and tossed away the magazine he'd been trying to read. She didn't seem surprised to find him there. "Celine, you might think about letting the past go."

"Oh, sure. You've had everything. Everything in your life is lined up in neat little columns. You can afford to 'let things go.' But this is all I have, what I built my life to do. I'm set to do that survey, Tyrell. I've got all the information I need."

"My life is not exactly neat now," Tyrell returned, because Celine was definitely making him feel illogical. Fearing losing her, he had to touch her, to know that she was safe, to feel that magical energy she brought with her into his life.

Miss Magic walked to the bed and flopped back on it. Then she curled on her side as though shielding herself from more pain. "I'm pooped. Lock the door on your way out. I'll remember to lock the door from the office next time."

Tyrell tried to shake the cool anger that was wrapping around him. He was certain that a locked door couldn't keep him from her. "I thought we'd have a chat. You need someone to talk to. You can't run away from the truth, Celine. Let me help."

"Me? Run away? Think again. You're the enemy, or didn't you know? I just had to go get a spare tire for my pickup. I did not run away." The bed squeaked beneath her as she flipped over to glare at him. "And why would I tell a Blaylock anything? All that kissing— You're getting desperate, now that I'm set to start an actual survey and have all the facts to work with. How does it feel, knowing that your money is financing the rightful owner and that isn't a Blaylock? Kissing was just a way to get to me, wasn't it?"

"It truly was," he admitted. He'd wanted to hold her and make love to her and the need grew every moment. Especially with her lying on his grandparents' lovely old bed. She moved again and the soft flow of her breasts jarred his instincts to take her.

Her glasses glinted at him, and her expression stated that their moods were not in alignment. "Because I'm a Lomax and you're a Blaylock."

"Oh, hell, Celine. Give it up." Tyrell wished he hadn't exploded. He ran his hand through his hair and glared at the one woman who had ever unnerved him. In fact, he couldn't remember a time when he wasn't in control—until Celine.

"You just yelled at me, Blaylock. Boy, are you ever typical. Someone challenges you over something and you get all rattled, male ego and all that. You get all defensive and shaken and clearly, you're delicate and emotional.... Don't look at me like that," she said imperially and sat up to jerkily unlace her boots. As she bent, her blouse exposed the deep crevice of her breasts.

Tyrell closed his eyes against the enticing sight and when he opened them, Celine was studying him. Her crossed arms served to lift the distracting portion of her anatomy. "What's wrong? Don't you feel well? Have you taken your temperature?"

"My temperature is fine and I do not yell. My ego is just fine. I'm just lovely," Tyrell answered and forced his hardened body to walk out the door.

The next day, Tyrell tried to ignore Celine and failed. She'd decided to wait to survey until she had more information from the neighboring landowners. He had yelled again when she'd bent over to collect papers in front of him. He had yelled because he'd been drooling over a woman who didn't care for him, and because while watching her round, soft bottom, he'd spilled coffee in his lap. She'd hurried to crouch and pat his jeans dry and had found him aroused. "Oh!" she'd whispered in a surprised tone as he glared down at her and wrapped his hand around her wrist, holding her hand away.

"Yes, 'oh.'"

"Someone is in a snit," she said knowingly when she dragged her eyes away from his hardened body. "And it isn't me."

Later, as she stood on tiptoe to reach a pad on the top of the office shelves, her long, tanned legs gleamed in the sun. Her shorts hugged her bottom and it jiggled as she stretched higher. Taut across her breasts, the thin T-shirt material etched every curve—Tyrell stood, walked to the shelves and easily reached the pad, slapping it down on her desk.

That afternoon, Tyrell almost toppled over in his chair as she entered the office from the garage. In a short black skirt and sweater and wearing gold hoop earrings and midhigh heels, Celine acted very self-conscious and yet determined. She sat at her desk and scanned her checking account, which Tyrell knew had to be low. As was her habit, she twirled one of those spiraling red-gold ringlets around one finger and Tyrell wished he could reach out and fill his hands with the silky, brilliant mass.

He caught the scent of her bath soap, and tried to concentrate on the numbers lined up before him. After four tries to make sense of the figures, he sat back and studied Celine. If Channing and Neil were circling Celine, Tyrell would call them out. A man who usually dismissed irritations and proceeded with logic, Tyrell felt just broody enough for a good brawl.

Just there, just below her left ear, was the tasty, tender bit of skin he longed to nibble. She stretched and her breasts lifted high. He could almost feel that softness cupped in his hands; his body jerked into alert. "When are you going to start that damned survey?"

"We both know that you're my only customer so far and that I need money. My dollar cushion is flattening by the minute. I've been doing some searcher work at the courthouse, but I'd rather be outside and tearing at the Blaylock ownership. This is called the setup, Tyrell, before I take your precious land away, and I'm doing lots of thinking about how I'm going to tell you that I'm right.''

''Fine. Think about this,'' he said a heartbeat later as he cupped the back of her head and leaned down to kiss her, not shielding his hunger. Her arms went up and around his neck, and as she matched his hunger, dragging him over her, Tyrell instantly gathered her closer. He ran his trembling hand down her smooth leg to the tender spot behind her knee.

He caught her uneven breath in his mouth, filled his senses with her sweet, restless sounds and placed her carefully back on the desk. He allowed his fingers to dive into that frothy silky mass of curls, his body to press against her softness. The delicate, ragged sigh that escaped her throat excited him even more. He was just foraging for that fragrant bit of her neck when Celine pushed at his shoulders. ''Um, Tyrell? Hi, Dan and Logan, Rio. James, er, ah, Roman.''

''We—'' James had to stop chuckling to continue. ''We thought we'd ask our baby brother to help load lumber for Logan's new house addition, but he seems to be busy.''

''That I am. Go away.'' Tyrell wasn't letting her get away, not after the first taste of her in two weeks. He slid into the desk chair and pulled her onto his lap. He was mildly surprised when she didn't try to struggle free. Instead she sat very straight and crossed her arms over her chest in a defensive position. He frowned at his brothers and tried not to tremble as Celine smoothed his hair. ''Get out,'' he said levelly to his brothers who were already laughing.

''I've got a unique photo of Tyrell at three.'' Roman grinned at Celine. ''I'll show it to you, if you like.''

''He was pretty,'' James said and dodged the eraser Tyrell had sailed at him.

''He *is* pretty,'' Celine said quite seriously, taking the box of paper clips that Tyrell was preparing to throw at Dan. She placed them firmly on the desk and looked at the Blaylock brothers. She looped her arm around Tyrell's shoulders as if they were good buddies. He moved her hand down to his chest, over his heart, and placed his hand over hers as she defended him. "But you shouldn't pick on him. I'll have to protect him if you bother him again. He's been sensitive lately, extremely moody. He's uncertain about his life. Trust me. You wouldn't like what I can do. I've lived with men all my life. I know that a certain powder in underclothing can cause men discomfort. Itchy shorts do not a happy man make. And, I'll speak to your wives. They won't like you picking on him, either."

Tyrell and his brothers stared at Celine who was not smiling, her lips slightly swollen from his hungry kiss. Then his brothers began to grin.

"I've been taking care of myself for a long time, honey," he said carefully, stunned that she would protect him. He was also uncomfortable with his brothers' close attention to the minor war. As the youngest of the brood, he'd had more than his share of brawls and wasn't exactly a daisy.

"You don't seem to be doing a very good job. Excuse me, please." Celine stood very properly, tugged her short skirt lower, smoothed it over her hips and walked elegantly from the room.

"You're drooling again, baby boy," James noted dryly as Tyrell tilted his head to one side to get a full view of her backside and long, elegant legs.

"Hey! Blaylock!"

Tyrell smiled as the rock hit his mountain cabin's wooden door. On a Saturday midmorning, late July lay warm and fragrant on the mountain, the wild roses blooming, the berries ripening and a summer storm gathering around the mountains, summoning strength to rage and tear. The moody day equaled Tyrell's unsteady emotions.

The clean smell of fresh lumber filled his cabin, the new bathroom addition essential to the woman he wanted to share his life. Packing the porcelain fixtures up the mountain had not

been an easy task, though he'd needed the physical strain t
keep him from chasing Celine down and making love to her
He wanted her to come to him, a little bandage on his dente
emotions.

"Blaylock! I know you're in there. These two pack mule
and that horse didn't just wander up here!"

"Hark! My sweetheart cometh to me," Tyrell murmured a
the second rock hit the door and bumped off the porch. He pu
down his hammer and waited, arms crossed. He'd wanted he
alone, here with him, without interruptions. "My fair Celin
wore a dress and earrings at the office. Every time she cam
near me, she was all big green eyes and curiosity and she wa
definitely in a nervous-female mode. I take that to be a goo
sign."

The next instant, fair Celine jerked open the door an
tromped in, her spiraled curls bouncing and shimmering aroun
her head with each step. Her hoop earrings seemed to glov
amid the vibrant curls. She slung her backpack onto the table
Her green eyes flashed, ripping down his bare chest and stom
ach, taking in his worn jeans and moccasins. "You know
camped two nights on the mountain and that I went down t
town to talk with some people. I'm still doing base researcl
hunting for old markers, and I can't find what I need, Cutter'
house. You slept just outside my campfire every night. I kno
you were there. I'm one person doing the work of three an
it's going to take forever—"

She caught her breath and glared at him. "Stop grinning
Your face is all stubbly and you look like a pirate. You can'
just do things like that, Blaylock. You can't just give me th
prettiest doll I've ever seen, all wrapped in tissue and dresse
in a lacy bridal gown, and wearing your grandmother's garne
necklace. You can't just put it on my pillow with a bouquet o
wildflowers and roses wrapped in a pretty handkerchief. I'r
not Miss Long, Tall and La-Di-Da, you know. I've never had
nor expected anything near so pretty."

"Then it's time you did. The handkerchief was my grand-mother's, too. She held it with a bouquet just like that when she married my grandfather." Tyrell noted the darkened areas under her eyes, the pale tone of her skin. She'd had a sleepless night before deciding to storm up to his castle. He'd had nothing but sleepless nights and staying with Else only emphasized his need to make his own family—with Celine. He wanted her in his life and in his bed; he wanted to provide and protect and share with her, and Cutter's lies stood between them.

"I'm a little old for dolls, and it's my first one. Wouldn't you know that a Blaylock would be the one to point that out?" Celine muttered darkly.

"It was a message from me, Lomax. I'm trying to be romantic. Try to stop talking long enough to decode the obvious," Tyrell said, pushing her onto a chair so he could bend and unlace her boots. He wanted to give her babies, not dolls. He crouched before her, tugged off her boots and rubbed her feet.

He pulled off her socks and studied the two small delicate feet in his hands. His body hardened immediately at the silky skin and his senses lurched as she wiggled her toes. His mouth went dry and his entire body tingled. Entranced, he moved his fingers over the delicate skin covering fragile, tiny bones.

"Wake up, Tyrell. This is me, Celine Lomax. Romance isn't what men think about with me. I've always been one of the boys."

"Trust me. You're not one of the boys." Tyrell allowed his gaze to flicker over her body, the light T-shirt covering her breasts, the twin taut buds rising to thrust at the cloth.

She stared at him and the froth of reddish-gold curls seemed to shimmer as if alive. "That's, um, unusual, the way you're touching my toes. You are a strange man, Tyrell Blaylock."

"I am around you," he agreed roughly, standing up to push his hands into his back pockets. He wanted to protect her and

couldn't. "I used to be logical, then you entered my life. Did
you find what you wanted?"

He ached for her, because he knew about being driven, about
the pain that came with it. She couldn't give up, and while he
admired her, he also knew what she would find would tear her
life apart. "Did you find anything to prove Cutter right?" he
repeated, and disliked himself for pushing the pain at her.

Tyrell realized that he was hurting, too. A man's lies stood
between Tyrell and Celine and she was fighting for those lies,
not Tyrell and the future they could have together. He was too
angry, not trusting his emotions. Only Celine had the ability to
unbalance him.

She paled and looked away, and instantly Tyrell knew that
Celine had found more to tear apart her belief in Cutter's lies.
"I took time to visit some people. I stayed overnight with them,
as you well know," she said very quietly. "They knew Cutter.
I asked some questions. They answered them thoroughly. They
said you'd let the word around that if I wanted information
about Cutter, to talk with me and tell me everything and the
truth—in the easiest way they could. Even the gentlest way
was not easy. I doubt that they would have spoken so freely
if you hadn't asked them to. Jasmine and the valley are a very
close-knit community."

The shadows in her green eyes deepened. She'd been torn
apart by Cutter's black lies, and Tyrell hadn't been there for
her. A slice of pain shot through him, his frustration adding to
his helplessness as he watched her destroy her beliefs. He
couldn't stop her, but he could hold her and listen—if she'd
let him. She had refused comfort from him. "I see. I would
have gone with you. You could trust me, Celine."

"No, I can't," she whispered. "Everything was so simple
and now it's not. I work alone and always have. I've survived
by being independent and tough. This necklace belongs to
someone who is a lady with a gentle, good heart. Mine isn't.
I haven't lived a sweet life. I'll return the handkerchief later."

She stood and held out his grandmother's necklace to him, the old gold chain and setting gleaming richly with the blood-red stones.

"I want you to wear it for our wedding," he stated carefully, studying her as he took her hand and eased her fingers around the gleaming Blaylock heirloom. "Take me and forget the rest, Celine. Let it go."

Her lips trembled, her expression wary and sad. "A Blaylock and a Lomax?"

"A man and a woman." Tyrell uncurled her fingers and lifted his grandmother's treasured necklace to place it around Celine's neck. When she shook her head, resisting, he took her face in his hands and smoothed the fine, freckled skin. He caressed the silky skin over her cheekbones and lost himself in her dark meadow-green eyes. In his heart, Tyrell knew she would be the only woman he'd love. Could she leave the shadows and trust him?

Her hands settled on his wrists, her eyes sought his— "You wore that skirt for me, that day, didn't you? And the earrings?"

It was a small concession to his pride to know that she would dress for him, thinking of him.

"No. Of course not. They were just something I found at a thrift shop.... Okay... Yes," she admitted after a pause in which Tyrell's heart seemed to stop. "You make me feel—"

The high mountain wind hurled against the cabin and the door slammed shut, startling Celine. She jerked herself away and tore out of the cabin. He found her standing on the porch, the wind whipping at her hair, lifting it up and away from her face. Her body leaned into the wind as the brewing clouds ignited with a lightning bolt. This was a strong woman, the other half of his heart, his life. Thunder rocked the air, vibrating the rough boards beneath his feet. Wind swept across the pines and firs, bending them, hissing savagely through the branches. His heart leaped within him, the primitive elements sparking his own darker emotions, needs that he'd kept close and safe and now tore from his keeping—

'"You are a woman. You should feel like one. It isn't wrong, and neither is this—" Tyrell jerked her to him, found the same primitive elements within her flashing eyes, the proud lift of her head, the taut set of her body. Words were useless now, just the emotions storming between them remained, as fierce as the natural elements brewing on the mountain. All the heat he'd need in a lifetime, all the passion, was there in Celine. She pushed her hands against his chest and he gloried in that resistance. If she took him, it was because she had thought through her needs and she wanted him. Celine's honesty was unshakable and he trusted her. Then her fingers slowly fisted his shirt, tugging him closer. There in the swirling thunderstorm and the pelting rain, he took her mouth as he'd wanted, open and fierce, slanting and hot, and the furnace of her own matched his, her arms lifting to lock him to her. Her hands slid to his hair, tethering him to her, her mouth and tongue as desperate as his own, matching him in a harsh, fiery hunger.

Tyrell swept her up into his arms, carried her into the cabin and snapped the lock behind him. In the shadowy room, with the rain pelting the windows, the thunder rolling as if to break the world apart, Tyrell looked as fierce as his ancestors, primitive, stripped of his leashes. Raindrops glittered on his skin, his shoulders and arms bulged, muscles ridged and defined beneath the smooth skin.

Instincts told her that only she had seen this man, that he had released this part of himself to no other. He trembled, holding her high in his arms, heat burning the cloth separating their bodies. Beneath those glossy long lashes, his eyes locked with hers. His dark skin taut upon his cheekbones, his jaw set and his lips burned beneath her fingertips. His chest rose and fell raggedly, his breath sweeping unevenly across her cheek.

While the mountain storm crashed and threatened outside,

Celine's body burned more than the summer heat and the earth-shattering sound wasn't rolling dark thunder; it was her own heart. He lowered her to her feet and stood apart, waiting as lightning lit the room, the stark fierce stance of a man who could take easily, but who waited for her. She knew the choice was hers: to become his and he to become hers. Making love with Tyrell would be no light matter and there would be no turning back. In Tyrell lurked a primitive emotion that echoed within her. A tremor ripped through his tall body and she knew he held himself tightly, waiting—

She took his hand slowly, raised it to her mouth and kissed the callused, broad palm. She heard the hiss of his indrawn breath, sensed the tightening of his body and saw the fire leap in his eyes. She smoothed the sleek strands of his hair, rumpled by her fingers, and placed her hand on his taut cheek. She saw what she needed there, the hunger and fire that matched her own. Taking care to ease her T-shirt up and over the old neck-lace, she undressed before him and pushed away the need to cover her body.

Tyrell's black gaze tore at her body, flowing down, then up to study her burning face. She knew that Tyrell would hold her gently, would travel slowly and safely into lovemaking. She forced her arms down at her sides and held her head high in the shadows of the cabin. The storm outside was no more fierce than what raged inside her. His light touch moved slowly from her throat to the necklace, circling it briefly before continuing down her body. His gaze followed his hand, dark against her pale skin. He skimmed the indentation of her waist, the gentle swell of her stomach and lower. The intimate age-old placing of his hand over her femininity startled her and she trembled, fighting the impulse to run. "I want this, too," she whispered shakily.

"Celine…" he murmured unevenly and she found herself swept high again as he carried her to the bed and placed her upon it. She watched him undress, almost a solemn ceremony.

He gave her time to change her mind, to turn him away. She couldn't; she'd waited for this moment all her life. He came to her, easing her between the sheets scented of him, and joining her carefully, lightly, and the trembling of his body told her how badly he wanted her. His rugged face burned against her throat, his mouth parted, hot upon her skin. He slowly drew her close to him, fitting her against his body so gently that she felt cherished, prized and feminine as he sighed raggedly, man against woman, woman completing man.

He'd asked her to marry him; with him, she felt like a woman. She felt needed like a woman.

His open hand trembled as it moved slowly over her back and over her bottom and down her thigh. His face nuzzled her hair as she slowly, uncertainly eased her arms around him, locking them together. Against her body, she knew his desire, felt it; in response, her body softened, heated and dampened.

He turned her carefully, drawing away the sheet to look down at her, his open hand sweeping lightly down her breasts, her stomach and lower, cupping her briefly before moving on. "You're so hot," she whispered as his touch burned a path over her body.

"You're very soft," he whispered against her breast.

"You're shaking." She smoothed his powerful shoulders, the muscles and cords rippling, quivering beneath the heated surface.

"I know. So are you." His lips burned her nipple, then the other, the gentled heated suction causing her body to quiver and lurch. He stroked between her thighs, causing her to melt and ache as Tyrell shifted, moving over her.

Braced upon his arms, lying over her, he smoothed her curls away from her face. "Afraid?"

"Not of this." She trusted him to take her gently.

"Of me?" Lightning from the storm lit the harsh features of his face.

Her fingertips traced the jutting, high line of his cheekbones.

"Yes. Of what you want apart from this. Marriage terrifies me. Is lovemaking always like this? So wild and frightening?"

He smiled tenderly and she relaxed a bit beneath him. She trusted his gentle touch, the violence he controlled for her. Tyrell kissed the sides of her lips, brushing across them back and forth. He seemed so comfortable and Celine moved slightly, adapting to the heavy masculine pressure pressed so intimately against her. She tensed as he began to enter, but Tyrell's mouth caught hers and hunger leaped within her. She held him tight, not wanting him to escape and the length of his body trembled, telling her how much he fought his own need so that she could be introduced to her own passions.

Then he nibbled her lips and desire surged within her, her hips lifting, her hunger causing her to cry out. Gently Tyrell eased slightly inside, then deeper and she caught her breath, terrified and shocked by the intimacy and yet hungering for him. His large hands stroked her body, his face against her cheek, his breathing hot and ragged as he kept himself from entering her completely. He tensed, holding her near as he reached beneath the mattress for protection.

Celine barely breathed, her eyes locked with his. Even now, Tyrell sought to protect her when she would have hurried on. She smoothed his hair as he came back to her, wanting him close, shocked by the insight that without his care, they could be making a life, a child between them. A miniature young Tyrell—wild and free with glossy black hair and laughing eyes—came dancing into her mind, just for a heartbeat before the fever ran on like a hot, raging river.

The wild, sweet, dark words he spoke against her throat urged her on, caused her blood to rush and pour and heat until her body was his and his was hers. Then he bit her shoulder, just a nip that surprised and shocked her, enough to set off the tightening constrictions within her. She cried out as he slid, full length and deeper, and rested shakily, his heart raging against hers. She held him locked to her, fearing he would leave and that she would tear apart. And there in the dark, shadowy room with the rain tearing at the windows, she stepped into the fire with him, set her lips to his shoulder and her fingers dug into his back, locking her near. The gentle rocking of his body told her that there was more, the violent beat of his heat urged her on and then the rhythm became fierce and wild. She soared freely, wonderfully into the colors that burst within her. Heated by their passion, the gold and garnets seemed to burn her skin, marking her as Tyrell's woman.

With her fingertips locked to his shoulders, her teeth against his skin, she knew her power as a woman then, the softness that he craved, the heat that he needed, that she needed, could be found within herself. The eternal woman, the strength that made her both strong and feminine, swirled around her, crystal clear within the storm of their passion. In that moment, held on that tight prism of blinding color, she possessed; she was possessed in equal measure.

In the distance, beyond the tightening of her body, she heard Tyrell's ragged, muffled shout match with her own and the pounding fire began to lessen into a sweet, drifting warm cloud.

As their heartbeats slowed, Celine found a peace she'd never known, stroking Tyrell's hair, winnowing her fingers through the blunt texture. Tyrell seemed to struggle within her grasp, as if trying to lift himself away and failed. She smiled against his damp face and he raised his head to take a hard, brief kiss before sinking down again heavily, his hand cupping her breast possessively. "Celine," he murmured against her throat as if he'd found everything he needed.

She loved his possession, the gentle stroking of his fingers, his weight sprawled on her, a magnificent man who trusted her. His touch reminded her of a fire, its hunger briefly fed and waiting to spring to life at the slightest breeze. Tyrell was more of a storm, she corrected, a very hot, passionate storm. She stroked his broad back and let herself drift in the peace she hadn't known before.

The erotic tugging at her breast matched the gentle seeking of his hard body. Celine awoke to Tyrell's body sliding into hers, filling hers and igniting her desire. She tore at him then, fought him and fought herself, crying out as passion seared away her fears and she moved into the storm once more. The burning height was more than the first, lifting and tossing her higher until she tightened and burned and let Tyrell's body carry her across the golden threshold until she drifted safely in his arms.

"This certainly isn't like my first time in the back seat of a car," she heard herself murmur, and slid into sleep with Tyrell's smile curling against her cheek.

Eight

Tyrell ducked the falling branch and pushed through the storm to check on the horse and pack mules. Thunder and lightning at midnight matched his savage mood, his anger at himself. He'd wanted no barriers between Celine and himself before they made love that first time. Yet, with her in his arms, he could no more resist her than the beat of his heart, the air he needed to breathe. Cutter's lies still stood between them, the age-old feud still alive and bitter.

He whipped the hair from his face. *He'd hurt her. Her body had tightened with pain and later, he'd tasted the tears upon her cheek.* He should have protected her from his passion, and waited for her to adjust to being a desired woman. He slashed away the rain from his face; he was glad that she couldn't see him now, as he really was—angry at himself for taking her, for taking what he needed. *If he would have stayed, he would have taken her again.* With Celine, he lacked the control that had served him all his life. He hadn't taken time to ease her into this relationship, into lovemaking, with traditional romantic courting. She should have had more—all the sweet things a woman treasures from a man's seeking of her. Tyrell's fists clenched tight. Instead he'd taken— She'd be too tender now, so small and tight as he'd entered her. Tyrell shook the streams of water from his face and welcomed the cold pelting rain to dampen the fever in his body.

His instincts told him to place his baby within her keeping. His instincts told him that his time had come to claim a woman and begin a family. They were primitive instincts, ones he'd locked away, but Celine had dragged them back to life. He wanted his child, a baby with Celine, in his arms.

The horse and pack mules were sheltered in the barn, greeting him with snorts and nickers. He gave them grain and stepped out into the storm, wanting to step away from shelter into the wild mountain storm.

"Get back in the house," he yelled as he saw Celine hurling toward him in the meadow lit by lightning. He was terrified for her, running toward her. She seemed so small and fragile, clad only in his wet chambray shirt, which tangled at her thighs. Pushed by the wind, the wet cloth outlined her curved body; Tyrell shook, riveted by the elemental sight of his woman caught in the storm, the other half of his life. Wind swept her hair, pulling it away from her face, her body fully defined from her breasts to her stomach and the V between her thighs.

"No, I won't go inside, until you do." Her hair was wet and waving strands clung to her face. She pushed away the arm he tried to wrap around her, to hurry her back to safety. "You look like hell," she stated flatly, almost pleasantly, reminding him of the woman who worked and spoke to men on their terms.

Celine resisted the slight shove he gave her back toward safety. She pitted herself against him and in his lifetime, Tyrell had never dealt with a woman he loved and wanted to protect.

He could hurt her now, with his veneer torn away, his emotions riding as wild as the mountain storm. Wind and rain hurled around them, wrapping them in a silent battle. "Leave me alone," Tyrell ordered and instantly regretted his threatening tone.

"Is it that you're sorry? That you wished you hadn't mentioned marriage—this lovely necklace?" She wasn't frightened, but pushed forward into her own fears. Her fingers pressed against the heirloom on her throat, glittering in the lightning and rain.

"This is how I feel about that." Tyrell tore away the wet shirt, leaving Celine nude and pale and gleaming in the rain, the necklace her only garment. He traced every curve, desiring her, fearing her, loving her. "I want you now, just like I always will. I wanted to wait, to let you adjust to marrying me, but I couldn't control myself. Not with you. I took, and I hurt you. I wanted to give you more."

"More? There's more? But that's great, Tyrell! Is that what this is about? Why are you fighting me? Because you're afraid you hurt me?" With a husky, rippling laugh, that seduced and beckoned, she hurled herself at him, locking her arms around his shoulders, her hands fisting in his hair. She pushed her face against his and licked the rain from his lips. She bit his lip and hurriedly kissed the slight wound. "If you're sorry, I'll kill you."

"Not a bit. You're what I want. My woman. You fill me. But I wanted to give you more time." The verbal expression was macho, possessive and old-fashioned, but as true as his emotions for her. She was woman to his male instincts, the woman he'd wanted to give his child, to grow old with and to cherish.

Pale in the blaze of lightning, her expression challenged and raged to match the storm. "Take that back, Tyrell, until you're honest with me. You've been holding out on me, but show me now what you feel. You know my life. Tell me what hurts you so, or don't say that I'm yours.''

He should have expected that fine temper and the threats. Less than an hour ago, she'd lain soft and sweet in his arms. Now she looked furious, ready to fight him with words and punches. He wasn't certain of how he would react tonight, in the storm with her temper flying high at him. Fearing for her, he tried to tug her away, to protect her against the savage emotions running through him. Then unable to resist, he wrapped his arms around her and buried his face in her throat. ''I should have come back,'' he admitted roughly to the other part of his heart. ''I found out later how badly my parents needed me, needed what I could do for them. My father called and I knew something was wrong. He wouldn't tell me that he and Mom almost lost everything due to a bad crop year and a second mortgage, and I didn't come home. My brothers and Else helped. I didn't. I was too filled with myself.''

Her hand smoothed his face and that odd settling eased over him, despite the fierce storm crashing around them. ''Shh. Your parents would have wanted you to do what you wanted.''

He shuddered against her, terrified that in his need to hold her, he could hurt her. ''I was too busy...too damned busy to be bothered.''

''Are you too busy to be bothered with me...now?'' she asked gently, challenging him.

He mopped back her wet hair and clasped her close to him, sheltering her. His hand smoothed a round bottom, and found her breast, cherishing it. ''You'll catch cold, and it will be my fault.''

''Yes, it will.'' She leaned back to smirk at him and that delightful dimple tore him away from his guilt. She fluttered her lashes at him. ''You'll have to wait on me, and be my slave. Boy, will I make you pay. I can be a beast.''

Then she placed her head on his shoulder and snuggled close to him, her arms around his waist. Tyrell couldn't move, trapped by his racing emotions. She'd followed him out into a raging storm, faced him at his worst and had reached inside to soothe him.

There in her arms, the old pain was gentled and swept away by a need that Tyrell sensed would never end. He picked her up and ran through the rain, carrying her to his bed where she belonged.

"His woman. Tyrell Blaylock's woman." Sunday night, Celine opened her hand to study the garnet necklace that had been Tyrell's grandmother's. The dark red stones, old filigree settings and heavy chain, rich with age and love, gleamed in her hand. Carefully fitting the necklace to her throat, Celine faced the woman in the mirror.

She turned to one side and pushed back the heavy ringlets, arching her throat until the gemstones glittered on her skin. She looked almost like a pagan goddess, and definitely a well-loved woman.

The ripe tenderness in her body reminded her of Tyrell's alternate gentle and fierce loving.

Waking up to a half-naked man with a brand-new rag doll draped over his shoulder had been a new experience. That morning, she'd been grateful that Tyrell was dressed and cooking breakfast when she awoke. The rag doll propped against his shoulder and held in place by his chin was at odds with his masculine bare chest and the dark stubble on his jaw. He'd been back in control and had tossed the doll to her as she blushed and tried to look sophisticated at the same time.

Tyrell had smiled tenderly. "The doll is for you—from me. You should have what you need from life.... The basics in the bathroom are working fine. Take your time, honey. Breakfast can wait," he said as if they'd lived together for years.

"Tyrell? Don't you think I'm a little old for dolls?"

"Nope. Besides, I had fun just thinking about your expres-

sion right now. It's a cross between a pleased smirk and surprise, and honey, it's definitely revving my motors.''

A woman. She really felt like a woman—feminine and soft
and treasured. She'd have to give the necklace back, of course.
It belonged to the Blaylock family's heritage and now Tyrell
had placed the beautiful necklace that had been Garnet Marie's
around Celine's throat. "Don't even think it has something to
do with land or money or revenge or payback," he'd whispered
close to her ear as he'd fastened the necklace around her throat.
She was no more stunned by the gift than by the sweet, lin-
gering kiss he'd given her as if he were giving her a part of
himself.

She ran her fingertips over the necklace, warm and rich on
her throat. The stones seemed to burn, coming alive to her
touch, the gold gleaming. Just for tonight, before she returned
the gift to Tyrell, she'd wear the jewels. Celine tugged away
her usual T-shirt and practical bra and stood in her cutoffs and
bare feet. Quickly she stripped away the cutoffs and panties
and stood looking at herself, wearing only the blood-red stones.
All the essentials were there. Woman-female essentials. She
turned her back to the mirror and studied her curves. Just that
flash in Tyrell's dark eyes as she raced to the bathroom draped
in the sheet told her that his desire had not died.

"I'll have to think about this," she'd told him shakily over
the pancake breakfast he had cooked. She was uncomfortable
with a man caring for her, a man who had loved her so pas-
sionately there in the bed just feet from her. The man in her
life definitely desired her, yet he treated her as an equal, not a
servant as her father and grandfather had done. "I'm not sorry,
but I just have to think. It's like the world is flipping over and
everything's changing right under my feet."

"I know," he returned with a wry smile that warmed those
beautiful eyes.

"I'm...sorry you have scratches on your back," she'd had

to say, ashamed that she had dived into the storm with him. "And that bite on your throat. And I think I'll go home now."

"Whatever you want. But if you want to stay, I could use a hand in setting up the solar heating unit for hot water. Then Else would kill me if I didn't pick blueberries for her muffins. And for your information, Miss Blushes, I'm proud of those marks you gave me. I see them as your contribution to—um, let's just say you aren't the kind of woman to take and not give."

He stroked a finger down the slightly reddened line on his shoulder. "I'm fond of these—my first."

"Really? You haven't...?"

"Give me a break, Lomax," he'd said easily and stuffed a forkful of pancake and syrup into her gaping mouth.

For some reason, the thought that Tyrell had never shared that heated a fire with another woman, pleased her very much. "I'm your first then, huh?" she'd asked around the mouthful of pancake.

He'd lifted an eyebrow. "Don't push it, honey. What happened before you is done and not up for conversation. We're not having a beer and boast session."

"Well, just tell me—"

"Lay off. Do you want to wash or dry?"

"How many?" she'd pushed, digging into Tyrell's past love life.

"Absolutely none as passionate or sweet as you," he'd answered smoothly, which delighted her.

"Tyrell, I think I should tell you that this experience was much better than my one-and-only. I was just a teenager, testing myself in a grown-up world. Johnnie was there and eager and I wanted to know the mechanics. In comparison, you were quite unique. And large. The defining boundaries—"

Tyrell shook his head and stuffed another fork of pancake into her mouth. "Spare me the ancient replay."

"I'm trying for 'the morning after' something-nice etiquette here, Blaylock.'' From Tyrell's darkening expression, she decided that his morning-after ideas ran more to activity than niceties. Moments later, beneath him, she knew happily that Tyrell was a man of action and instincts—not etiquette.

"I should be going,'' she'd whispered later in the mountain meadow filled with daisies. Tyrell's eyes had glinted that special way, his gaze softening upon her as he artistically tucked the daisies in her hair. He'd bent to nuzzle her neck and to rest against her for just that heartbeat, startling her. She'd held his head against her, wrapping her fingers in the sleek, sun-warmed strands, terrified and yet glorying that this powerful, controlled man needed her—and with her, he wasn't always controlled.

Looking at the woman in the mirror, Celine placed her hand over the elegant, glittering necklace on her throat. "It was all a dream—wearing this and riding bareback on Tyrell's horse to the site where he wants to build a house. He wants me to survey and see if a road is possible to that site. None of this is real. I just know it isn't. Not a Blaylock and a Lomax.''

A man and a woman, Tyrell had said. *His woman.*

She'd hadn't seen herself as a woman with tender emotions that Tyrell could tear from her. She hadn't seen herself as a woman reveling in her body, the pleasure and dreams—

Celine ran her hand down her bare hip, resting on the curve as Tyrell's large one had done. He liked drawing her against him, cuddling her, and yet she didn't think of cuddling when she held Tyrell close; she thought of tearing his clothes away and feasting upon him.

Well, not quite. She was shy of him and blushed too much, which seemed to delight him. "The role of a woman is a tricky thing. I mean,'' Celine said to her mirrored image, the woman wearing the garnet necklace and holding the new rag doll as if it were a child. "I mean, if I—or does he? Who makes what moves first? And this marriage thing. I really can't see that. Not me as a wife. As a mother.''

The thought terrified her. Her own mother had run away from a one-year-old child. What would she know about running a home, taking care of a family, living in one place and loving on a long-term basis? What were the guidelines, the boundaries, the markers? She nuzzled the doll and wondered about the intricacies of Tyrell's large body easing into hers, and the black-haired, beautiful child that could result—

"I'm sorry, Cutter, but my heart tells me to believe a Blaylock," she whispered, shaking with emotions. "All these years, you fed me so much hatred and now I'm learning to see how wonderful life is."

On Monday night, she studied Tyrell's face, lit by their campfire. "I can't pay you to help me."

Crouching in front of her, he unlaced her boots and placed them aside, then rubbed her feet. In the campfire light, he looked delicious, dressed only in his jeans, his hair and body still damp from his swim in the icy mountain lake. "I want this finished, Celine. Two can do the work better than one, isn't that right? I'm here and I want to help."

"What about your clients? All those whiz-bang deals you've got going? What about Mason wanting you back—there was a message on the machine—" She stopped talking when she saw his dark look at the mention of Mason's name.

"I'm here with you and I want this settled."

"You want to protect me, don't you?" she asked as he turned to check the fish baking by the fire. "I've been in the field before, under worse conditions."

He turned to her. "There are rattlesnake dens here, cougars and any amount of danger, let alone one wrong step could start an avalanche or send you down a rocky canyon. In two weeks, August will start to turn cold here in the mountains. I don't want you hurt or sick from exposure."

"You realize that no one has seen to my safety before, that I've managed quite well—"

"I'm not questioning your ability to take care of yourself. This is for my own peace of mind. We're in a relationship, sweetheart. I prefer to be by your side. You're the woman I want to marry and who I hope will someday want my children. Here—eat. I thought you'd like to clean up a bit before sleeping. Your water should be warm by the time we're done." Celine looked at the towel and soap Tyrell had placed beside the bucket of heating water. The wildflowers he had placed on the towel almost caused her to cry; she knew that he would never treat her less than cherished because the Blaylock men, once bonded, kept their loves close. She hadn't been loved; she didn't know how to return it.

That night, Celine looked at Tyrell, who had placed his sleeping bag near hers. She hungered for him, ached for his warm, hard body against her own. "Why aren't we—?"

He inhaled raggedly, his rugged face gleaming in the dying firelight. "We've complicated the problems between us and they need to be resolved. I want this finished, honey. You need thinking room. But I want you badly, if that's what you want to know."

"Oh." Then Celine couldn't resist placing her hand on his chest, to take a bit of his strength and to feel his heart race against her skin.

Tyrell took her hand to his lips and turned to curl his tall body around hers. Lying in the safe spoon of his body, Celine listened as he told her about his life as a boy, his mother and father loving each other, the antics of his sister and brothers and always the warm safety of a family. "That's what I want for my children," he said with a kiss to her temple. "Think about it. We'll work this through."

The first week of August Tyrell watched Celine take notes in her field book, listing the land description chiseled on the boundary stone. She sank to a rock, sitting with her shoulders slumped, her head in her hands. Tyrell moved toward her, then held himself in check. She wouldn't appreciate his comfort now, not when all the evidence denied Cutter's charges. After a week of carefully surveying Blaylock land, each marker had been in place as it had always been. Each day, she got quieter, that sassy mouth in a pale grim line, and at night he held her as nightmares stormed around her and then he damned Cutter for the life she'd led. Tyrell unballed his fists and inhaled and walked to her. Asking her for a romantic evening wouldn't suit her low mood, but a one-of-the-boys approach might. "I'd like a night off and a few beers. What about it?"

The casual invitation wasn't exactly the romantic evening he would have preferred, but Celine was more apt to accept it. "Um, sure. I could go for that," she returned dully after one searching look at the boundary marker in front of her. The chiseled inscription matched that of the Blaylock deed. Later, as he watched her sleep in his grandparents' bed at the gas station, Tyrell smoothed back her jumbled curls. He had planned to sleep at Else's, to protect Celine's reputation, and yet he couldn't bear to leave her alone. With the washer and dryer humming in the night, he undressed and moved into bed with Celine, curling around her body and drawing her back against him. For a time at least—he caught a flailing hand as she fought the past in her sleep—he could hold her the way he wanted to.

He awoke to a cold glass of water tossed in his face and Celine's furious expression. She was dressing hurriedly, tugging on her cutoff bib overalls over a worn T-shirt and stuffing clean clothes into her backpack. The rag doll was tucked into the front of her overalls, arms flopping as Celine moved. "You'd like that, wouldn't you? Me lying around here and not getting done what I have to do?" she demanded as she bent to lace her boots. "I'm taking this thing the whole distance, because I have to. I'm doing the survey—and about marrying you—you talked in your sleep, Blaylock. I heard every word. 'Marry me and forget the survey.' Well, I won't. That would be the easy way, wouldn't it? Marry the opponent. Typical, typical, typical. So typical.''

''I asked you to marry me,'' he'd shot back. ''It's not a takeover.''

''Isn't it? Isn't it, just? It seems to me that you're taking over my life—my only client is also sharing my office space, and sleeping at my campfire.''

''You're frustrated and taking it out on me and that is *our* campfire.''

''Mine,'' she said. ''Everything is just great. I'm not frustrated. I'm going to find some little tiny spot of evidence to prove Cutter right. But I can't do it with you as a distraction.''

''So I'm a distraction now.'' Tyrell didn't like feeling like a spare tire.

''A real big one,'' she said darkly and that admission soothed him a bit; at least she noticed him.

On the trek back to the mountain, Tyrell decided it was better if he didn't talk—he was too angry. She pushed him, ''To the left, hold the prism straight,'' as she focused the transit at the rod he was holding. And, the classic, ''Lasers can't do all the work, the people holding them have to know up from down.''

When she started the next morning with a, ''You intend to slow me down, don't you—taking all this time to prepare breakfast. Has anyone ever told you that when you're camping you don't need to deliver a perfectly cooked breakfast with bacon, eggs and hash brown potatoes? And then wash the dishes and pack them away, and then shave and—''

''The shaving was for you, sweetheart, to protect that silky skin. I wouldn't want to rub any freckles away when you come after me,'' he returned darkly.

Her eyes first widened, then narrowed, blazing at him. ''Me? After you? Freckle remarks will not be tolerated.''

''It wouldn't hurt if you showed a little affection, dear. And your freckles are all over that sweet milky skin and in the best places,'' he'd shot back at her, angry with his body for needing hers when she clearly was out for a fight. ''Let's get this idiocy over with and finish the job.''

''What? You're calling me an idiot?''

Tyrell ran his hand over the beard he hadn't had time to shave. Unable to stop himself, he reached for her T-shirt, grabbed a fistful of it and drew her up to her tiptoes. He took a hard, fast kiss, because he had to, and then said in his best even tone, ''Let's just get this done, okay? And for the record, I don't give a damn about the land or the feud you keep gnawing on. If you're trying to get to me, you just did. But the offer of marriage stands. I've come to love freckles. On you. I'd like a little girl with them and curls, but chances are we'll have boys and they'll look like me. Too bad. And with any luck they won't have their mother's hot temper.''

She locked her fist to his T-shirt and he tried not to wince. ''That's hair under there, sweetheart. Let go.''

''You let go.''

''Aargh!'' He released her shirt and Celine released a delicious smirk up at him. Tyrell was horrified to find he'd raised his arms in a gesture of frustration. He clamped them down to his sides and walked away with as much dignity as he could manage.

When she finally talked to him again at noon, she fired him.

In return, because they were both yelling, he ordered her off his mountain and that if she persisted, she'd be trespassing. At that, she tromped off into the woods and returned a few minutes later to finish the argument. By this time, Tyrell was swimming nude to cool his temper and his desire.

''Okay,'' she said, throwing the words over her back so she wouldn't look at him. ''You can work for me. It's just that you're so emotional lately.''

''Gee, thanks,'' he muttered and decided to swim across the lake and back to trim his frustration and his need of her.

By the second week of August, Tyrell's patience was exhausted. They worked well together, sharing camp duties, but

Celine could be maddening, distracting, enchanting and sweet. One soft look from those sultry green eyes and he was aching and hard. Day by day, he watched Celine's quest crumble, her spirits drag and there was no way to stop her, to protect her from the truth.

He suspected that Celine's deep sense of loyalty battled with her shredded past, with her absolute belief in Cutter. A woman like Celine loved with all her being, and held hope with a clenched fist. While those traits were her strength and how she had survived, now they were her weakness. She'd built a lifetime upon her love and belief in Cutter and it would take time to heal. At times, she simply sat, staring into space, and he knew she was seeing the past and Cutter through new, questioning eyes. For a loyal believer like Celine, the journey would be torturous and slow. A thorough woman, she'd reexamine each incident and lie, balancing it, taking it into her and facing what she must do—for herself.

Meanwhile, just watching her take in the truth, replacing the lies, was almost unbearable for Tyrell. He knew that he couldn't make Celine's journey for her, but that didn't help his frustration.

The survey was completed when he ripped off the payment from his checkbook, walked to her desk and plopped it down. He picked up the completed survey and walked back to sit and glare at her. "Let's not talk for a while, okay? And don't even think about returning my grandmother's necklace. The survey may be finished, but we aren't," he warned, turning his attention to the accounts he had neglected in pursuit of his lady love, who was scowling at him and hugging her rag doll instead of his baby.

He picked up the ringing phone, listened to Mason babble apologies and promises to "prosecute the woman who started this mess." Tyrell knew that Mason needed to blame his mishandling on someone else. He studied Celine's curious expression and answered. "I'll call you back."

Mason needed to place the burden on someone else for his mistakes, and Tyrell would not have Celine be the scapegoat. Tyrell intended to make certain the question never came up again, but first he had to visit Celine's mother, Elinor—he had to understand why she had left her daughter. Cutter had lied about everything else, and if there was any chance he could protect Celine and discover why she had been left with Cutter, he would.

When he hung up the line, he turned to Celine. "I'm leaving. You run from what's happening between us, and I'll find you."

Her chin went up, green eyes flashing. "I've never run from anything in my life."

"I knew I could count on you. I always can, and that's why I love you."

"My brother isn't easy to understand, but you seem to be doing a good job of it," Else said as she poured afternoon tea into cups. She wrapped a clean dish towel around the brown pottery teapot, one that had been in the Blaylock family since homesteading days. The teapot almost whispered of woman-to-woman talk, something that Celine had seldom experienced. Else pushed a giant square of cinnamon-scented applesauce cake toward Celine, the aroma blending with that of the mint tea. An experienced cook, Tyrell's sister checked the bread dough rising beneath an embroidered tea towel.

"He's gone," Celine said around the mouthful of delicious cake. She studied Else, uncomfortable with sharing her thoughts with another woman. She missed Tyrell; he'd dropped an "I can count on you" and a "love you" on her and walked out the door, leaving her. His expression had been too hard, restless as if he were already centered on a project ahead of him, reminding her of how she'd first seen him on that New York sidewalk. The incredible emptiness of him walking away from her tore at her; she'd wanted to run after him, but pride kept her locked still. He'd come back, she knew without qualms. Tyrell was a man who kept his promises, even in anger—and she'd tried her best to nettle him during the survey. She'd been fighting herself, her need of him, and the terrifying knowledge that Cutter had not been truthful. Tyrell was very different from the men in her family. He'd been her friend, she realized now, ready to listen just as Else was doing now. Celine ached to hold him, to have his arms around her, to place her head on his chest and listen to the steady beat of his heart. "Tyrell just ran off."

"Men and boys," Else said in a tone that promised to understand, a wise tone of a woman who had experienced her share of brothers, a husband and male relatives. "Tyrell is the same as his brothers, yet different. They are all individuals, and yet have the same qualities beneath it all. Our parents never got the chance to tell him what they needed to before the accident."

Else ran her finger around the rim of her cup. "They felt they made a mistake with Tyrell, that they'd pushed him too hard. A teacher came to the house one day, Tyrell's math teacher, and told my parents that he was exceptional and that he needed more math and science classes. At the time, it was only a small school without advanced placement courses, and too far from a college to help. No one here had a computer back then. My parents agreed to him taking correspondence college courses really early—he must have been around fourteen or so. They thought it was best for him, and he became too serious, trying to please them. It seemed he was always traveling to some math contest or another, and bringing home awards. We were all proud of him. But our family didn't just love him for what he could do, we loved him for himself."

She sighed and raised her apron to wipe away a tear. "Dad said Tyrell didn't need anything but the mountains to make him happy, that of all my brothers, Tyrell was a throwback to our mountain man ancestor, Micah Blaylock. But my parents felt they'd pushed him too hard, into something that ruined his chance for happiness. He was just a happy boy and then, suddenly he was too serious and fearing failure. They wanted him to have Micah's wilderness to match what ran dark and controlled inside him. I wish they could have seen him now with you, alive and steaming.''

Aware of the dark sadness in the other woman, Celine placed her hand over Else's. ''You should tell him. He feels badly that he wasn't here. Your father called him to come home.''

Else frowned. ''Dad called him to come home?''

''Tyrell thinks that he should have been here to help with your parents' financial trouble. He thinks he could have made a difference.''

''Dad and Mom went through a bad spell, but we all pitched in, just like they did for us all the time. Now, that is high-handed of my baby brother, isn't it? To think that we couldn't manage?''

Celine recognized the trademark Blaylock pride in Else. ''Tyrell needs to be needed,'' she said softly. ''You should tell him what you told me.''

''You're saying we cut him out, all of us. That we made him different by trying not to bother him,'' Else said slowly, thoughtfully. She studied Celine. ''You're good for him, and us. He's really stirred up now, not a cool, calculating machine. It's something to see after all these years.''

Celine blushed. ''He is a bit of a…mmm…he's not always serious. He likes to tease.''

Else's eyes widened. ''Tyrell? Teases?''

She glanced at the door where Hannah, Kallista and Paloma had just entered. ''Come have some cake and tea.''

Within a half hour, Celine learned that she'd missed a great deal in life by not having women friends. In the next hour she learned that women did say ''butt,'' usually preceded by ''gorgeous'' when referring to their husbands' anatomies; they didn't like some aspects of housekeeping and disdained dirty diapers as much as men. These women weren't dainty and fearing outdoor life; they liked sunshine and battled just as fiercely when they believed in their rights. They liked dressing up to watch their mates' expressions and they liked being cherished and treated like lady loves.

In the second hour, Else banished Joe from the house; she brought out worn poker cards and chips. Kallista called Roman with orders for Kipp's nap and Hannah called Dan, saying she would be late and he'd have to manage on his own. Paloma smiled at Rio's tone. "You'll get along fine without me for an hour or two. I'll make it up to you, honey," she purred and winked at the other women.

"He's so easy," Paloma said when the call was finished. "Raise the bet two toothpicks," she added, reaching for another square of applesauce cake.

Celine's afternoon with the Blaylock women proved to be revealing. The women's opinion of Tyrell was that his male ego was wounded and that he needed petting and protection. Celine could manage him quite nicely with a few feminine tips, which the Blaylock women supplied. "He's a hardhead," Else said, clearing away the poker chips and cards. "Mother always said he would be the worst one—" She looked at the other women who were groaning in disbelief. "She did. She said he holds his emotions too close, unlike Rio. And she said that once he found a woman he wanted, he'd carry her off just like Micah Blaylock did the first bride in this valley. The problem is, Tyrell is a bit hampered by society's laws today, and I'd say he's frustrated."

"Men are delicate creatures," Celine stated thoughtfully and was surprised when the other women laughed.

"Don't tell him that, but it's the truth," Paloma agreed.

"It's our secret," Hannah said with a finger raised to her lips. "Men need to feel like they are big dangerous creatures. So we let them feel that way."

"You know I'm a Lomax," Celine had to say.

"I'd say that you've got some hard miles behind you. You'll find the truth of what you seek, but meanwhile you need something that helps you think. Something to do when the quiet hours come at night," Else said thoughtfully. "You've got a home now, you've made a home, and you need time to think. This is what you need—" She placed a big wooden embroidery hoop and a basket filled with embroidery floss in front of Celine. "This was my mother's and it was Grandmother Garnet's. Think and embroider and come back to visit. I love my little brother and you're good for him. I like that and I will talk with him."

"Thank you," Celine murmured, and prayed that Else could ease Tyrell's needless guilt.

"It's I who should thank you," Else said warmly and bent to give Celine a kiss on the cheek. The women shared a look, and at that moment, Celine knew she had found a rock-steady friend to last her a lifetime.

Nine

"**A**nything for the cause," Tyrell said and slapped a big, weighty sealed envelope on Celine's desk. After a week without her, and drained by traveling in August heat, Tyrell tried not to act stunned when he entered the office. He tore away his dress tie and realized it wasn't that tight; his body was. Dressed in a simple, short light flowery print dress that flared above her shapely knees, Celine looked like a cool, very feminine oasis. Held back from her face with twin combs, her spiraling curls tumbled in a saucy, longer arrangement; the tiny dangling citrine beads at her earlobes added a flouncy, feminine effect.

Off balance by her delicious, shy and welcoming smile, Tyrell was tired and nettled by the discovery of another Cutter lie: Celine's mother hadn't left her; Cutter had run off with the baby while Elinor was working. It took Elinor two exhausting years to find Cutter and Link, only to be told that the baby had died. He'd produced a death certificate, saying the baby was cremated and her ashes thrown to the wind.

Tyrell wasn't certain if he could leash the need to kiss Celine's enticing lips, a reassurance of sweet truth and innocence. He was in a rough mood, filled with storms and terrified for Celine and how she would react to the news that her mother was alive. "I want this finished. The information in that packet will help."

Presenting her with the diamond engagement ring now in his pocket should have been first on his agenda to marry Celine; it wasn't. The past could rise at any time to destroy whatever trust she had in him.

Celine's green eyes were too soft and wounded, and Tyrell shoved his hands into his pockets, feeling as if he'd slapped her. She hadn't asked why he'd been away; she'd accepted his absence, a sign that she expected the men in her life to come and go as they wished, without explanation. Tyrell didn't like his comparison to her father or grandfather, but he didn't want to explain his mission to uncover her past. Celine was proud of her ability to deal with her own problems.

Then there was Mason. Filled with apologies, Mason wanted Tyrell back. A series of telephone messages, oozing with promises, meant nothing. Mason threatened to come out to Jasmine, possibly with Hillary, who could identify Celine from their brief encounter. Mason and his daughter were capable and unpredictable troublemakers, ready to rake up any dirt to get what they wanted.

His friends had said Mason was desperate, the business failing and each move he made—some of the moves shady—had created worse problems. Mason was volatile, quirky and underhanded when he wanted something—and he wanted Tyrell back.

How could Tyrell tell Celine about her mother, now in Iowa? His research, begun immediately after Celine's dramatic appearance on his land, led to Elinor Drake. Elinor had never stopped searching for her lost child until she found Cutter, who served her a lie. A wonderful woman, she had remarried, and

Celine had two half-sisters. Link and Cutter had made Elinor's life unbearable, and when she decided to leave, they'd run with one-year-old Celine. Elinor's picture of Link was that of a weak son, goaded by his bitter father.

Tyrell ran his hand down his rough jaw, the scrape of stubble against his palm matching his unsteady emotions. He understood Celine's drive to succeed, to prove the Lomax claim. Though she didn't know her mother, Celine was an exact replica, and many of her actions, twirling her curls as she thought, were the same. He wanted to pick her up and love her, to protect her from the past. But he couldn't; she deserved to know everything and Tyrell did not like feeling as though he had betrayed her, reaching out to find her mother.

He wanted to reach back in time and destroy Cutter and Link.

"You look all dark and broody, as though you want to kill someone. What's this?" Celine asked, her fingers smoothing the big battered packet.

"Open it." Tyrell sat at his desk and punched the button on his message machine. He didn't listen to the messages, he was too absorbed in watching Celine. The swaying citrine stones at her ears caught the sun dancing against her skin. The muted print of her dress only emphasized her femininity, the soft fabric flowing away from her long, tanned legs, and snuggling against her breasts. Sunlight danced in her hair, the ringlets longer than when they met, her hands lightly touching the deeds and journals as if they could burn her. The old documents had long been in his family, from Micah Blaylock's claim to the land to a copy of his parents' split of the old homestead to their children, and they proved true everything Celine had set out to prove false. A fighter, she'd find the truth and face it.

Then, when she could face another hardship, he'd tell her about her mother. Celine had lost a lifetime with a good, loving woman. There would be no way to retrieve those lost years.

Celine's life had been built on lies and pain, and Tyrell ached for her.

He ran his hands through his hair and down his unshaven jaw. The old records would deepen her pain. He couldn't bear to watch her shatter. He spoke roughly, his emotions dark and unsteady. He wanted to protect her from men like Mason and her grandfather. "I'd like you to marry me, Celine. No matter what you find there, the offer stands."

"You realize what these could do, Tyrell," she said quietly. "Old journals sometimes reveal more than deeds."

"I do. You're obligated to make good your threats of taking away Blaylock land. I'm going up to the cabin. The wonder of battery operated electronics will let me handle any emergencies from my clients."

She glared at him. "Hard week?"

The insinuation that he'd been with another woman pleased Tyrell's dark side. He leered at her. He hadn't leered that much in his lifetime, and realized that he'd probably done his share around Celine. "Very hard."

He took pleasure in that emerald flash of her eyes, the way her freckles danced across her face before she seemed to ignite; her hair gleamed like a torch, picking up the light from the window.

His intentions to finish the problems between them ended with Celine's dark, sultry look. After a week away from her fire, Tyrell had to go to her, take her face in his hands and take the kiss he needed desperately.

"Let me know how it comes out," he said against her mouth before gently biting her soft bottom lip. If he didn't leave soon, he'd want more than a fiery, hungry kiss.

"You'd trust me with these? Your family records?" she asked shakily.

"I'd trust you with my life," he said, meaning it. He tried not to stare as the hem of her skirt slid higher on her tanned thigh. He could almost feel that slender-strong feminine leg move beneath his hand. Tyrell forced himself back to the path he had chosen for their relationship, the traditional one she deserved. He considered himself to be a saint as the hemline slid higher. "How about dinner and a movie on Saturday night? You'll have a whole week to prowl through those without me around."

"Just like that? You've been gone for one week and come back on Monday looking like a worn-out tomcat. You kiss me as if you're starved, and then you plan to stay away another week and *then you want a date?*" she asked, her voice rising and trembling with anger.

"Did you miss me?" He prayed that she did, that she ached for him as he had longed for her.

He couldn't resist trailing a fingertip down her hot cheek. Celine wasn't as dispassionate as she pretended. She expected more from him than from her grandfather, and Tyrell took that as a good sign. "Jealous?"

"Maybe I've got plans for Saturday night," she returned levelly with a toss of her head. "I just could be discussing ripping away Blaylock land over a nice candlelit dinner, with an attorney."

He admired that fire, the feminine way she smoothed her hair and the way she shielded her shredded emotions. She was letting go of a lifetime of lies and pain and just discovering her power as a woman, a fascinating transition. He'd give her more time to adjust and then he'd tell her about her mother. He toyed with a ringlet, fascinated with its silky texture and fiery color. "You just remember to wear my grandmother's necklace at our wedding, sweetheart. When you're finished with those, give them back to Else. I already know what's in them. And by the way, I know of a good financial advisor, if you're thinking about investments."

"Ooo," she steamed as he walked out the door whistling.

"Typical," he said, smiling as something crashed against

the door behind him. Whatever Celine felt for him, it wasn't lukewarm.

September's fiery falling leaves slashed against Tyrell's cabin window as Celine stirred the stew. Wherever Tyrell had been in that week, he'd returned troubled, frustrated and wary of her. In the times he had worked at the office, he'd been efficient, slashing his pen across papers, already impatient to be away from her. At times, she would find him studying her, sadness in his beautiful black eyes.

She spoke to the puppy lying on a braided rug and happily chewing on Tyrell's moccasin. "Give me that. He's being a real rat about this. Setting up a date, acting like a perfect gentleman, when I know he's not, parking by the lake with me and kissing me senseless, only to take me home without—just without. For a logical man, Tyrell should know what is logical after a dreamy date like that. And then, to give me that hope chest he'd made in the week without me. It's a beautiful big thing, all smooth oak and brass hardware. He made me a gift to last forever, the beast. He knows that I've never had anything so wonderful."

The Blaylock journals and deeds proved they had purchased their land with the sale of Texas cattle, crops and sweat. Cutter's stories were spiderweb fragile and shredded, and now she desperately need to see Tyrell. "He knew all along and gave me time to understand—"

She peered out into the slashing cold rain. "Tyrell is out there. It's just so typical for a man to be thoughtless when dinner is almost ready. He didn't know I was coming, but I had to see him. Someone has to take care of him, roaming around this mountain like a lone wolf."

She glanced at the old leather-bound book placed next to Tyrell's computer, the red ribbon bookmark old and frayed. "My Diary" Garnet Marie had elegantly scripted across the faded leather front. Cutter had spoken softly of Garnet Marie, as if he treasured her. Though Celine did not know what was in the diary, she knew that Garnet Marie's words and thoughts would be lovely and genteel.

Celine closed her eyes against the pain that went skipping through her as she remembered her grandfather's bitterness toward Luke Blaylock. She traced the old diary, written by a woman from long ago. The Blaylocks treasured their grandmother and each other, unlike her own family. Celine glanced out into the slashing rain and it reminded her of that first time with Tyrell, how gentle he'd been, fearing for her. Neither one of them were casual people, to go on as if nothing had happened. Each time she looked at him, her heart leaped and an infinite warmth spread throughout her.

The old deeds and journals that Tyrell had given her provided a strong picture of the Blaylocks, of the strength of the family. She couldn't find mention of Cutter's cabin, nothing but people building lives and raising families and loving each other. Tyrell's life was so different from her own. She would have to leave him, of course, because she had no other clients, or reasons to stay in Jasmine. She would leave him because she would not fit into the fabric of his life as a Blaylock. She didn't know about families or how to be a mother, how to fit into the steady, day-to-day life of a married woman. She didn't know how to share her life, how to stay in one place. "That hope chest was meant to stay in one place, in one home forever and to be passed down to daughters and sons. I can't possibly pack it all over the world with me when I'm working, and he knows I can't bear to leave it behind."

Celine took off her glasses, needed for distances, and picked up Garnet Marie's embroidery hoop. She smiled whimsically, thinking of how much she had changed, taking time to embroider pillowcases. She smoothed the imperfect first stitches of a flower and thought of all the women in the Blaylock family who had filled their hope chests while dreaming of future husbands.

She inhaled unevenly. If there had been a single valid indication that the Blaylock land was rightfully Lomax, she would have been forced to act—or could she have? How could she tear dreams away from the Blaylock family, from the women she'd grown to love? Did she know how to love, rather than hate? Weary from days of battling the old journals and feeling that she had failed, Celine picked up the embroidery hoop and needle. "If that ornery lone wolf doesn't come home soon—sexy telephone calls every night just aren't the same thing—I'm going after him. He could be hurt. That would be just typical of him—to give me that beautiful handmade chest, planed from timber on his land, when he knows I don't have a thing to give him in return."

Tyrell cursed, every muscle aching, as he walked up the log steps to the cabin. Breaking a new gelding and riding him across the mountain suited Tyrell's dark, raging mood. He was cold, bruised and weary clear through, desperate to hold Celine safely in his arms. She had to work through her past; devastation awaited her and he was helpless to prevent her pain. He was angry—at Cutter and Link, and himself for not handling Celine more gently, for making love to her too soon. "She deserves her dreams. Like some half-brained love-starved teenager, I had to hurry to the finish line before she knew what was happening. So much for control. It wouldn't surprise me if she leaves. I made her cry with that damn bridal hope chest and what did I do? Walk away. I don't know how to handle her. One taste and I'd—"

Celine deserved to know about her mother and the burden fell to the man who loved her.

Under the porch now, he slapped his wet Western hat against his thigh and noted the light in the window. "Must have left the generator on. I'm not thinking straight anymore."

Else had cried. His sister was a strong woman, and the sight unnerved Tyrell. She'd told him that Celine had made a dif-

ference in his life, in all their lives, and that the Blaylocks
hadn't been fair to him, that his parents had wanted to tell him
so much before they died. Maybe someday, he'd—he'd needed
Logan's brute of a gelding, unbroken and roaming the wild
highland pastures. Flashback had been free since spring and
Logan believed that the untamed horse was different, deserving
a bit of freedom before winter and hunger forced him down
into the valley. Flashback didn't like being trapped in a wooded
corral, or ridden. Pitted against each other, man and beast,
they'd ridden across Micah Blaylock's hunting and trapping
lands, the wild mountains that would soon be covered by snow.

And every minute, Tyrell ached for Celine. His helpless feeling grew as Celine's search wound closer to the pain waiting
for her.

He shoved open the door and slammed it behind him. Instantly a puppy started yipping; the light brown dog lunged at
Tyrell, snarling as he sank his teeth into wet jeans and began
to tug fiercely at the intruder. The enticing scent of food surrounded Tyrell at the same time he saw Celine on his bed,
dressed in his flannel shirt, and struggling to awake. The impact
was enough to make his knees weak—everything he'd needed
in his lifetime smiled shyly at him, her tousled curls framing
her sleep-flushed face. One pale shoulder escaped the red flannel shirt she'd borrowed and the upper curve of her breast
beckoned.

Tyrell glanced at Garnet Marie's diary, fearful that Celine
may have read the worst about Cutter. Afraid of his rough
emotions, his joy at finding her and his fierce need to take her
on his bed while she was warm and soft from sleep, Tyrell tore
off his wet coat and tossed it aside. She could think he'd betrayed her, searching and finding her mother—perhaps he had,
and he didn't like being part of more pain. "What are you
doing here?"

The question slashed at the air between them.

Celine blinked at him sleepily, and blew a curl from her face.

Her shy smile slid away, replaced by a challenging expression. "I don't know how to embroider. So what's it to you. You can't just come in here in an evil mood and start yelling."

The statement stunned him. Once again off balance and uncertain of himself, Tyrell thought of all she'd faced in her life, of what she would face and of the life she'd lost with her mother. She'd built her life and occupation around Cutter's lies and now she worried about embroidering?

"You know what? You're typical. An emotional, illogical female." His emotions warred with each other; he wanted her desperately, yet the past had to be resolved in her mind. This was a woman who matched him and because he was feeling bruised, he lashed out at her. "I'll thank you not to meddle in my life, like telling Else about Dad's last call."

"I'm learning how to meddle and I like it. I've discovered that I like being a woman. Do you have any more problems?" She smirked prettily and that expression knocked him breathless.

"I'm thinking." He sat and stripped away his damp boots to find the puppy attacking his socked feet. He reached down to rub the puppy's ears. "What's this?"

"Someone dumped him on the road out of town, can you imagine?" Celine asked, drawing the quilt up to her chin. "I thought you needed a friend. Because if you don't stop growling, you might not even have him, and he can be bought for puppy food."

Tyrell studied the small brown puppy who would eventually grow into a very large, hungry dog. The puppy had already torn a hole in his sock. "Help. I'm being attacked," he muttered, wary and uncertain of how he should treat Celine. He reached down to pet the puppy again, who promptly chewed on his hand and then flopped over for a tummy rubbing. Tyrell studied Celine, her wide eyes, and her blush that told him she was thinking of making love with him. "If you smirk, I'm done for. Now, why are you here?"

Silly, he thought. He wanted her to tell him that she loved him.

The next thought slammed against him and his body went cold. *Was she leaving? Had she finally given in to the truth?*

Celine pushed her curls away from her face in a way that caused his mouth to water and his body to harden. His mouth could almost taste that silky skin of her throat, just there behind her ear. She smoothed the quilt over her legs. "I thought you might know how to embroider. I'm too embarrassed to ask anyone else. Then after I realized that Else probably had you at her disposal when you were younger—"

Tyrell groaned. "Say no more. Yes, I know how to embroider and if you tell my brothers that, I won't be held responsible. Sometime between five and six, I was ill and in bed for weeks. That's when Mom and Else ganged up on me."

He knew if he came near her, he'd be lost. Her fragrance was filling his senses. In his raw, dark mood, fearing for her and feeling helpless, hating what her grandfather had done to her, Tyrell was uncertain of his control. "I'm eating and taking a bath. If you know what's good for you, you'll get out of that bed."

"Oh, I know what's good for me," she said when he returned to the room to find her snuggled in his bed, the room dark. In the shadows, she smiled at him. "You could come over here," Celine whispered softly as the puppy yipped around his feet. "Where you'll be safe from the puppy and you could teach me about embroidery, and—"

Tyrell was moving toward her, stripping away his jeans, his only clothing. He stood near the bed, wanting her too much, fearing his need. His heart stopped as she slowly lifted the blankets for him, an invitation he could no more refuse than breathing. Tyrell eased into bed, sitting upright as Celine was doing, the embroidery hoop in her hands as she watched him. "Sit closer," he said, needing her against him. "The better to see, my dear."

Once Celine's warm soft body snuggled next to his, her head resting on his shoulder, Tyrell began to embroider. His mind wasn't on the stitches, but the soft warmth of her body, her bare breast against his arm. He eased closer to her, almost groaning when both soft breasts pressed tight against him. She traced his hand, much larger and rougher, as the needle moved in and out. "So that's how the flower petals are made."

"French loops, and don't ask me to show you how to crochet an edging to the pillowcase." His leg burned at the soft, sleek stroke of hers. He turned to look at her dark green eyes and found a hunger that matched his own. He placed aside the hoop, noted the puppy fast asleep on his rug again and slid down into bed.

"I'll bet you know how to crochet that edging," Celine said as she snuggled close to him.

She kissed his shoulder and Tyrell tensed. "So you missed me?"

"Only this much," she whispered as she eased over him. "Feeling better?"

He lay very still as she nibbled on his throat; she'd given him more than he'd ever hoped. He blinked, stunned, as Celine's hand slid low on his body, curling around him.

"Uh!" Celine grinned, thrilled, when Tyrell flipped her over, his body pressing down on hers. He'd come from the cold, looking dark and angry and shaggy, and he certainly wasn't cold now, his body burning, hard against hers. She'd made a difference in his life, and in doing so, had changed her own. She'd found a man unlike all others, one she could trust and cherish. Tyrell was larger and stronger, as he liked to point out, but in his way, he was sweet and tender. She gathered him close, easing him upon her, his rugged, rough face pressed tightly against her throat. He quivered in her arms and she smiled again, realizing that she had created the need within him, the hardness of his body, and that of a man seeking shelter from storms. He sought her for another reason, a very private man, whose instincts told him it was time to take a woman.

She smoothed back the strand of hair crossing his forehead. "You know I can't haul that hope chest around the world with me, though I love it. You'll have to keep it for me."

"I wanted you to have something I'd made." He bent to kiss her eyelashes.

"I'm not exactly an old-fashioned woman, Blaylock. I had no idea that women used to embroider and quilt and place pretty tea towels in a chest for their married life. I have nothing to give you in return and I don't like unbalanced odds."

"Mmm. You'll think of something," he answered huskily, nibbling on her throat. "But it's not a trade-off. I just wanted you to have something I'd made for you."

She traced his eyebrows, sleek and warm beneath her fingertip. "What's bothering you, Tyrell? Are you missing the fast pace, the challenges of high finance?"

He snorted at that and when her fingertip came close, nipped it. "Let's stick to the challenge at hand. Why did you come up here?"

She grinned at him and pressed a kiss into the hand that had come to ease her curls from her face. "To learn about French loops."

"I'm doomed." But his smile was tender upon her, his kiss aching and hungry.

She stretched luxuriously beneath his body, all hard angles and muscles, and sleek black hair against her breasts and lower. She arched and reveled in his need, in what would happen between them.

Celine smoothed Tyrell's broad shoulders as he braced above her; she traced the hard muscle on his upper arm and slid her hand to his back where the taut skin rippled beneath her fingertips.

"What are you doing?" he asked roughly.

"Surveying. Checking out the territory." She could trust Ty-

rell to respond perfectly as his trembling hands swept possessively down her body, digging slightly into her hips, lifting her
against the stark power of his body. She needed to be locked
to him, burning in the fever that went beyond the moment, that
bonded them in other ways. She would never hold a man like
this, never trust one, as she did Tyrell. "This is for me," she
whispered, opening for the blunt masculine pressure as she
skimmed her parted lips across his shoulder.

Tyrelll's uneven groan proved his desire and unsteady emotions—he'd tried to protect her from his needs and that she
could not allow. He sank deeply into her as she knew he would,
and she received him moistly, tightly, arching higher. Tyrell
shuddered, his body taut and hot against hers, and against her
ear his whisper was desperate. "Why?"

She kissed his shoulder and raked her nails lightly over his
back, causing his body to ripple against her. "Because I know
that look. You're determined to be gentle and slow, and you're
not getting your way, not now. I need everything, Tyrell. I've
waited so long to be a woman with the right man, the only
man."

Uneasy with her admission, she trembled as his mouth slid
to her breast. "Is this your spider to the fly act?" he asked.

She smiled, bending to kiss his cool damp hair. "Some fly.
You must weigh— Oh!" she cried out as his lips closed upon
her breast and his hands began to stroke lower. She locked her
arms around him, finding the rhythmic heat pounding them,
taking them higher. Her body clenched, holding him tightly, as
Tyrell's mouth sought her other breast, his body deep within
her.

Gently he eased her legs higher, filling her. She gripped him
closely, arms and legs, matching his kiss, slanting her mouth
to give him better access, taking him deeper until the tempest
swelled and shattered. Above her, Tyrell's expression reflected
the primitive emotions of a man set upon one course, completing her, his honed features sharpening, his mouth slightly

swollen from her own. Her vision blurred then, the red-hot haze filling her, pounding at her, and with a cry against Tyrell's mouth, she knew that they had bonded, man and woman, as they were meant to be.

When she floated down to earth, Tyrell's large hand gently cradled her breast, her body held tight and protected against his. She continued floating, reveling in his soft touches, those kisses along her cheek, the slowing of his heart against her body. His hand splayed across her stomach and she knew that he was thinking of a Blaylock child, one she could not have, prevented from the past between them. She watched him ease away the tangled blankets to look down at her pale body, twined with his hard one. "You're so perfect," he whispered unevenly, the reverence in his tone slamming into her.

She smoothed his cheek, drawing his lips to hers. For a time, the short sweet kisses floated across her lips and then— "Tyrell?"

"This time is for me," he whispered against her ear. His lips moved down her body, suckling, nibbling and Celine launched herself at him, already meeting his hunger.

Sometime in the night, they made love again, gently, a bonding and a seeking. Falling asleep with her cheek on his shoulder, her hand on his steady heartbeat, Celine knew that whatever tormented Tyrell had momentarily been buried in his need of her.

"Stop smirking," he whispered sleepily against her forehead.

"Can't," she whispered back, happily nuzzling his skin, filling her senses with his familiar, dear and unique scent.

Ten

At daybreak, Tyrell leaned against the cabin's logs, holding the puppy. A sense of peace that he'd never had before surrounded him as he surveyed the mountain's mist hovering over the colorful aspens. The day would be cold and bright, steam coming from the horses as they grazed in the frosted field. Under Tyrell's woolen coat, the puppy shivered, cuddling against him. During the night Celine had cuddled to him, and Tyrell wondered if in his sleep he'd ever stopped smiling.

A soft, loving woman, bruised by life, slept in his bed; Micah's old cabin, deserted for years, was now filled with homey scents. Celine needed to rest, and Tyrell ached to protect her from the pain awaiting her. Celine had not spoken of Cutter's lies, she had only given.

In the canyon lay yet another pain, buried by brush and years, and when the time was right, he would show it to her. Tyrell inhaled the cold crisp air and wished he could tear Celine away from here and what she would find. He could try.

He might succeed; but she needed truth, and truth lay here in Jasmine and in the canyon and in her heart. He listened to her stir within his cabin and smiled as he thought of her deep in the bubble bath he'd prepared. It was a peaceful time, waiting for the woman he loved, waiting to see her eyes fill with him, waiting for that soft, shy smile.

A glitter of broken glass shot through the mist in the canyon like a spear. It reminded Tyrell of one more secret he wished Celine did not have to face. *How could he protect her? What could he say?*

Forty-five minutes later, Tyrell had given grain to the horses and stood again cuddling the shivering puppy. Behind him, the cabin door opened. Tyrell smiled as Celine's arms closed around him from the back. She was too quiet and the slight shudder of her body told him that she was crying. When he would have turned to hold her, she held him tight. A tiny sniff terrorized him. "Sweetheart?"

"I just read part of Garnet Marie's diary—don't curse, Tyrell. I couldn't resist. It was as if another woman called to me, wanted me to know something of her life. She was a beautiful woman, filled with love, and long ago, Cutter tried to hurt her with his brand of love. She chose your grandfather, Luke, the right man."

"I should have been more careful with Grandma's diary. Else gave it to me for you. I couldn't bring myself to read it. It seemed to be waiting for a woman to read it, not a man—" He damned himself for being careless, for being so excited at seeing her that he had forgotten to hide it.

"You kept it to protect me, didn't you? So I wouldn't see how awful he was."

"I thought she might have written about him. For a time, he was part of her life. Honey, let me hold you." *What was that sound? A cracking branch torn from a tree by layers of ice? Or was it his heart?*

She held him tighter, burrowing against his back. "Don't

you dare move. You're my anchor now, Tyrell, and I can't bear to release you, not even for a moment.''

He stood very still, with Celine resting against his back, her arms locked around him. He would serve her as she asked, though he wanted to hold her to soothe his own fears. Holding the puppy with one hand, fearing to move to put him down, he laced his free hand with Celine's. ''Better?''

''It's so beautiful here with the pines and the aspens and the stark trees— What's that glittering down in the canyon?'' she asked suddenly as the day shone bright and cold around them. ''Glass? I missed that the first time, probably because of the heavy brush in summer, but now—''

''Honey, don't—'' Tyrell took time to place the puppy in the cabin before hurrying after Celine. An athletic woman who ran quickly, she tore down the brushy slope to the old shack. Following her, Tyrell watched helplessly as she quickly circled the old building, taking her bearings from the mountains. The metal roof was bent and broken, pounded by fallen trees and age. With the expertise of a seasoned surveyor, she slowly scanned the location, aligning it with the jutting mountains. When she turned to look at him, her face was stark with pain and glittering with sunlit tears. Her voice vibrated in the freezing air, her body taut, fists clenched at her side. ''This is Cutter's 'fine, big house,' isn't it? And you knew all the time, didn't you? Tyrell, don't take one more step toward me. Not one. Stay away from me!''

Outside the executive offices of Mason Diversified in New York, Celine smoothed the slacks of her only basic black business suit. She pushed her curls back from her face. They were longer now, and she'd just discovered how much she liked the sensuous feel of Tyrell's hands in them, fascinated by his expression as he wound them around his finger. Because she would never see her love again, she'd hold his expression dear, the memory of his hands in her hair. She touched the gold hoops in her ears, a symbol of how much she had changed since meeting Tyrell. She didn't like running from Tyrell, nor could she run to him, a man whose career she had ruined. She'd tried to destroy his life and tear away his family's dignity and reputation. Now she intended to try to repair the damage to his life.

She faced the man who had been Tyrell's employer. Melvin Mason needed a good exercise program and less alcohol. "I want to correct a problem I created," she said. "I'm willing to pay for what I did."

To give Tyrell back what she had taken from him, she'd walk into hell.

Mason's eyes focused on the white T-shirt covering her breasts, and Celine impatiently tugged her jacket lapels together before continuing. "Tyrell is an honorable man. He's done nothing wrong. I had a, um, I had the mistaken idea that his family had wronged mine. When I saw the chance to take away his career and reputation, I took it."

"I see." Mason's tone insinuated that he knew of her actions against Tyrell. He rose from his desk to come around and sit in front of her. "You realize that you cost this company a major kingpin. The penalties for what you're admitting are extensive."

He placed his hand on her knee, his eyes narrowed behind his glasses. When she pushed at his hand, his fingers dug into her flesh. Celine did not hesitate. She reached for his ear and stood, holding it tightly. "You will listen," she said firmly.

Mason rubbed his ear and leered at her. "A fireball, huh?"

She began to pace the luxurious office, unconcerned with his insinuation. "I'll take any punishment due me. I want you to give Tyrell back his standing, his employee benefits, his reputation and anything else that was his before I interfered in his life. He's a good, decent man who doesn't deserve to have his dreams torn away. He's kind and gentle and loving—"

"Let me get this straight," Mason interrupted. "You love

him. You're going to bat for him. You'll do anything to get his life back where it was.''

"You've got it. He's sweet and honorable and—'' She glanced at the door where Tyrell had just entered, dressed in jeans and a denim jacket. He did not look happy. "You!'' she exclaimed.

"Surprise,'' he murmured darkly. "When I discovered you were missing, a quick check with the local airlines listed you as a passenger. I could only think of one reason why you would come to New York—you're in a cleaning mode, and only you would fly off half-cocked to finish something you started. You're like that—big on closure.''

"Tyrell!'' Mason exclaimed, hurrying toward him with an outstretched hand that Tyrell ignored.

He continued to study Celine, his day-old beard gleaming in the office light. "Get back to the part where you love me,'' he said too quietly.

"We can work this out,'' Mason said hurriedly. "Mason Diversified needs you, Tyrell. If this woman did tarnish your reputation and cause all this to come about, I'm certain our attorneys can find some way to make her pay. I can't just let her go unpunished if she's cost me a good team member—''

Tyrell continued to study Celine. "So here we are,'' he said. "You ran off, and you love me. Somehow the two don't seem to go together.''

She eased behind the desk as he took a step toward her, and shook off Mason who wanted to talk to him. "I'm 'kind and gentle and loving,' but you ran away,'' Tyrell prompted.

"I had to,'' she whispered, her throat tightening with emotions. She thought never to see him again, to torment herself with what might have been. "I think it's best.''

"You make the decisions for both of us, is that it?'' he asked in a hard, clear tone that raised the hair on her nape.

"What do you see in me?'' she had to ask, wondering how

this man could follow her, how he could have loved her so exquisitely.

His answer took away her breath. "Everything. I see my life, my future, my happiness."

Mason slammed his open hand on the desk. "Tyrell, you should be glad to get rid of this woman, and remember that Hillary has never once stopped believing in you."

"Uh-huh. Celine, the next time you get a harebrained idea to run off and leave me, remember that I'm not any more likely to give up than you are."

Just looking at Tyrell delighted her. "I'm sorry about taking your four-wheeler to the airport. My pickup wasn't working—"

"Car theft, too?" Mason screeched. "Good Lord, Tyrell, you cannot possibly be serious about this woman!"

Tyrell turned slowly to Mason. His next words were spoken like a promise he would keep all his life. "I am."

"We need you here at Mason Diversified. Let's forget this whole thing and go back to where we were. There are all those run-down companies that you used to enjoy picking up. They're just waiting for you to—"

"We're done." The terse words shot at Mason, whose face turned red with fury. Tyrell turned back to Celine, extending his hand to reveal the garnet necklace. "Are you coming home with me?"

She placed her fingers on the glittering stones, tracing them in his callused palm. "I can't. I feel too badly about what I've done. That day in the canyon when I discovered— I couldn't bear for you to touch me. I felt so unclean. You know that everything I believed in was a lie. Yet you came here to protect me?"

"I always will," he said, meaning it. He wanted to hold her close, but Celine had to make her own decisions. "After you found the—Cutter's place, I wanted to give you time to think, not run away, Celine," he added, noting his own frustrated tone. Leaving Celine alone to think, to wind through her past life and come to her own conclusions and decisions, was the most difficult thing he'd done in his lifetime.

"I did not run away," she stated, gripping the old necklace and lifting it to clip around her throat. "I'm sorry if I hurt you when I found that shack—Cutter's 'fine, big house.' I couldn't bear to watch your expression, as if your heart was being torn from you."

Tyrell placed his fingertips on the glittering necklace. "You are my heart. I feared for you. I didn't tell you, because I wanted to avoid hurting you even more."

"Garnet's diary left no doubt as to Cutter's actions. I should have known. I realized the details didn't match, but some small part of me—"

"Hope. We all hope, honey, you most of all because you're you, and you're loyal to those you love. You loved Cutter and you believed. The world needs more people who love and trust without reservation."

"I've closed the door to the past and to Cutter, Tyrell. I want a future with you. I love you, Tyrell," she whispered.

"I know. You had the strength to come through this and you completed the journey and didn't run from it. You're not a woman to love lightly, and you have the heart of me. We'll work this out."

"Yes, we will," Mason began. "We were a good team once and we will be again—" He closed his mouth when Tyrell slashed a dark, furious look at him.

"I had business to finish and I did not run away from you," Celine said firmly, delighted as Tyrell reached out to touch her hair in that exquisite reverent way. He could still care for her, after all that he knew about her and her family.

He looked at her as though he would cherish her forever. "You came here to protect me."

"Tyrell, someone has to protect you."

"Protect him? Ha! The guy is a combination of ice and steel.

You'd better worry about yourself and the trouble you've caused—'' Mason's muttering was cut short by Tyrell's step toward him.

Celine reached out her hand to touch Tyrell. She had to finish what ran between them, despite Mason's presence. When Tyrell's black glittering eyes turned to her, still lit by anger, she was almost frightened. But she couldn't lose the moment now to tell him everything. ''Back to what we were saying. You're so delicate and vulnerable. I love you because you're a gentle man, and because of all those wonderful things you're doing for people who can't afford your services, if you charged. You should be here, playing power games and— And I do love you. It's just that I am probably not the best woman— uh!''

''Delicate, huh? Remember that the next time you hit me.'' Tyrell had hitched her up to his broad shoulder. He walked out the executive door with Mason scurrying alongside them.

''Mmm. Typical. But it's okay. Rather sweet. I think I like this,'' Celine said, bracing her hands on Tyrell's lower back. She almost felt sorry for Mason who was near tears and begging Tyrell to stay and offering a partnership to him. ''No one knows him like I do. I really don't hit him that hard. I was a featherweight boxing champion and I pull my punches with him. He knows how to embroider and he—''

Tyrell's light swat on her bottom reminded her to keep more of a business position with Mason. ''I'm afraid he's made up his mind,'' she explained to Mason who had sunk to begging her to reason with Tyrell. ''He's an instinctive man, you know, and he's not in the mood to talk with you now. I really wouldn't push him. He is very strong and very dependable.''

''I'll find some way to make her pay for the damage she's done,'' Mason yelled. ''She walked right into my office. She admitted her hand in this mess that has cost me top people.''

Tyrell turned slowly to face Mason. ''My colleagues and

clients left this company because they didn't trust you. You'll have to rebuild, Mason. If you can.''

From his tone and taut body, Celine realized just how hard and terrifying Tyrell could be when challenged. Draped over his shoulder, Celine could not properly view the situation, but she felt Tyrell's big body tense warningly. Fearing that Tyrell would hurt Mason, she braced herself up and patted her love's taut bottom. "If you hit him, I'll have to protect you. He isn't worth it. Home, boy."

"Was that a 'yes'?" After a moment, Tyrell relaxed slightly, and she felt his control returning. He eased her from his shoulder into his arms, still carrying her out of the building. In the sunlight with people staring at them, Tyrell took her mouth with a hunger that pleased her.

"Yes," she whispered against his lips.

"I have a mother," Celine said slowly moments later as she finished reading the letter Elinor had written to her. She'd sensed that beneath Tyrell's hunger to kiss her, to hold her against him, he remained troubled. A terrifying urgency hovered around him as though he knew they had a journey to finish. She trusted him to take her anywhere, and he'd given her the letter on the way to the airport. This time she did not run from Tyrell, but turned softly into his arms.

They flew to Iowa where Celine met a mother who had never stopped searching for her. With the same red-gold hair, a little gray now, Elinor's joy was shared by her husband and Celine's two half sisters. "Could we keep her for a while?" Elinor had asked Tyrell as Celine cried upon his shoulder. "Just a bit?" Elinor questioned, stroking Celine's curls. "I've missed her so much. I'd love for you to stay, too. She's clearly in love with you."

Tyrell took Celine's fist, which was gently beating his shoulder as she cried and lifted it to his lips. "Whatever she wants."

"You're not going anywhere, Blaylock," Celine murmured against his throat. "I need you."

Epilogue

"**Y**ou!" Tyrell shouldered open the door to Micah's cabin and carried in his bride of one day. He placed her on her feet and dusted the snowflakes from her nose. "You wanted to come here when we could have stayed just as well at the gas station. It's late November, Celine. You're frozen clear through. I should never have let you talk me into this. The temperature is below zero."

"You were happy at the time you agreed," Celine managed through chattering teeth. "I've used snowshoes before and I've trekked in Arctic weather. We're wearing the best silk underwear possible and all the deluxe gizmos you insisted upon. We had no trouble at all with the snow. It was a wonderful way to start a honeymoon in that icy, glittery-snow wonder world, using skis and snowshoes. Stop muttering, Tyrell. Just think of the wonderful time ahead of us."

"If you don't catch pneumonia. Keep that down coat on while I build the fire." Tyrell turned and Celine took the backpack from him and removed the puppy, placing him onto the floor. Logo promptly raced for Tyrell's extra moccasins near the bed and began flopping one of them side to side.

"Now, Tyrell. We can't start building the house you want until spring, and the gas station is fine. Meanwhile, I love it here and so do you. There's enough wood to last the winter."

Tyrell scowled at her reasoning. "This time next year, I won't be so easy to push around. It's hard to say no to a bride of one day."

"For your information, I love the outdoors and this place as much as you do." She formed a kiss on her lips and fluttered her lashes. "You're so easy, Blaylock."

His look darkened and heated. "Tell me that a little later tonight, Mrs. Blaylock."

When the fire was blazing and the cabin began to warm, Tyrell stood, rubbing his hands over his face and glaring at her. She almost felt sorry for him, a new husband faced with a bride who wanted to spend her honeymoon in an isolated mountain cabin. Clearly worried about the threat to her, he hurried to make her comfortable, starting the generator for extra heat and light. He looked like a frazzled husband, worried about his family, and careless of his own needs. He poured puppy nuggets into a bowl and Logo dived into his food.

"I love you," she whispered softly and as always, the words jarred Tyrell, causing his heart to flip-flop. He stopped making the bed and turned to her, his bride, a strong woman who had come so far and fought the past to win. He knew she feared the future, feared that she wasn't "wife material," but the other half of his heart was perfect and complete now. She'd seen that her mother was as any other mother—a warm, loving woman, who had tried relentlessly to find her. Celine stood before Tyrell now, bundled in a heavy green down coat and quilted pants. "I'm getting hot," she said, smirking at him in that delightful, enticing way.

Quite simply, just looking at her made him happy.

He hadn't expected the black lacy underwear he found beneath the layers of winter clothing, nor his grandmother's necklace. His wedding and engagement rings glittered on Celine's fingers as she lifted her hand to smooth his hair. "We've come a long way, haven't we, sweetheart?" she asked tenderly.

"We have. You fill my life, you make me complete," he said, thinking that he would remember her forever this way, still shy of him, and uncertain of herself as his bride. As she unbuttoned his clothing, he bent to kiss her lips, tasting his future with her. There would be other times, he knew, when the primitive need would ease for her body, but for now— Tyrell lifted her up into his arms and carried her to the bed. "I should warm this for you," he whispered. "I should heat those bricks and wrap them in towels and—"

"You warm me," she returned as he placed her on the flannel sheets. She pulled him over her and nestled beneath him, her hands stroking his back. She tugged up the blankets to cover his shoulders and smoothed the rippling strong muscles. "I love you, Tyrell. I can't get used to saying those words. I feel a little thrill every time I say them, and hear you tell me, too."

"Mmm, so do I." He nuzzled her throat and smiled when she giggled at the play.

She stroked his hair, fisting it luxuriously as she studied the black gleaming strands against her pale skin. "You've settled the distance between your family, haven't you? You're much lighter now, and I haven't caught you brooding since Else said I was to stay at her place before the wedding."

"You changed my life, Celine." Tyrell was now at peace, especially when he heard his wife's husky laughter amid his family's. All the storms had settled and his search for peace had ended with Celine.

Her dark green eyes studied him. "Our baby will have lots of cousins and a secure home, won't she?"

"Babies, and more likely to be boys than girls, and they will be loved. Your mother will make a great grandmother.'' He couldn't resist easing away the black lace bra to the creamy skin beneath. Then Celine reached for him and in his hurry, he tore away the scrap of lace at her hips.

Stunned by his rough actions, Tyrell lifted the scrap in his hand, preparing to apologize to his new, sweet bride, the one he couldn't wait to make truly his.

Celine grabbed his shoulders, nudged her knee against his and eased him on his back. "Celine, I—"

Her kiss caused him to forget everything but the heat between them, the passion that sprang instantly to life, sharpened by abstinence before the wedding. Celine dived onto him, locked her arms around him. While Tyrell was adjusting shakily to being loved so enthusiastically, the smile beginning to spread all through him, she adjusted her body over his. Her thighs opened for him, her hips pressed down upon him, her heat enfolding him as he held his breath, stunned by her need of him.

As she eased upon him, taking him slowly, Tyrell smoothed her hips, their eyes locked with a lifetime promise that their bodies were already making. "I love you," he whispered, needing to tell her before he couldn't, before the fire took him.

"I love you," she returned, the woman who was his life, his love, his future.

Sunlight skimming across the snowy mountain shot into the cabin's windows. Half asleep, half already preparing to take his wife again, Tyrell luxuriated in the curvy, nude body of the beloved woman nestled against him. Celine had emotional battles to meet from Cutter's dark legacy. She would meet them and he would be at her side. He smoothed her breast and knew he should rise to stoke the fire to life. His thoughts rolled idly by and holding his wife in their first day of marriage was too sweet. She stirred, running her bare leg against his and before Tyrell could move, Celine dived under the covers to kiss his navel— "Hey!" he cried out, delighted, as covered by the blankets she began to kiss her way to his nipples. When his body jolted to alert by her mouth suckling at him, Tyrell tore away the blanket to find his wife's delightful smirk. "What are you doing, Blaylock?"

"Just doing my job. I'm a surveyor with territory to survey," she teased, before they began laughing and then loving.

*   *   *   *   *

Don't miss Cait London's next sensual love story,
LAST DANCE—the first book of FREEDOM VALLEY,
her brand new miniseries—on sale
April 2000 from Silhouette Desire
MAN OF THE MONTH.

LINDSAY McKENNA
continues her heart-stopping series:

MORGAN'S MERCENARIES
III
THE HUNTERS

Coming in October 1999:
HUNTER'S PRIDE
Special Edition #1274

Devlin Hunter had a way with the ladies, but when it
came to his job as a mercenary, the brooding bachelor
worked alone. Then his latest assignment paired him up
with Kulani Dawson, a feisty beauty whose tender
vulnerabilities brought out his every protective instinct—
and chipped away at his proud vow never to fall in love....

Coming in January 2000:
THE UNTAMED HUNTER
Silhouette Desire #1262

Rock-solid Shep Hunter was unconquerable—until his
mission brought him face-to-face with Dr. Maggie Harper,
the woman who'd walked away from him years ago.
Now Shep struggled to keep strong-willed Maggie under
his command without giving up the steel-clad grip on
his heart....

Look for Inca's story when Lindsay McKenna continues
the MORGAN'S MERCENARIES series with a brand-new,
longer-length single title—coming in 2000!

Available at your favorite retail outlet.

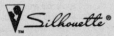

Silhouette®

Visit us at www.romance.net

SDMM2

If you enjoyed what you just read,
then we've got an offer you can't resist!

Take 2 bestselling
love stories FREE!
Plus get a FREE surprise gift!

Clip this page and mail it to Silhouette Reader Service™

IN U.S.A.	**IN CANADA**
3010 Walden Ave.	P.O. Box 609
P.O. Box 1867	Fort Erie, Ontario
Buffalo, N.Y. 14240-1867	L2A 5X3

YES! Please send me 2 free Silhouette Desire® novels and my free surprise gift. Then send me 6 brand-new novels every month, which I will receive months before they're available in stores. In the U.S.A., bill me at the bargain price of $3.12 plus 25¢ delivery per book and applicable sales tax, if any*. In Canada, bill me at the bargain price of $3.49 plus 25¢ delivery per book and applicable taxes**. That's the complete price and a savings of over 10% off the cover prices—what a great deal! I understand that accepting the 2 free books and gift places me under no obligation ever to buy any books. I can always return a shipment and cancel at any time. Even if I never buy another book from Silhouette, the 2 free books and gift are mine to keep forever. So why not take us up on our invitation. You'll be glad you did!

225 SEN CNFA
326 SEN CNFC

Name _____ (PLEASE PRINT)

Address _____ Apt.# _____

City _____ State/Prov. _____ Zip/Postal Code _____

* Terms and prices subject to change without notice. Sales tax applicable in N.Y.
** Canadian residents will be charged applicable provincial taxes and GST.
   All orders subject to approval. Offer limited to one per household.
   ® are registered trademarks of Harlequin Enterprises Limited.

DES99   ©1998 Harlequin Enterprises Limited

Desire

These women are about to find out what happens
when they are forced to wed the men of their dreams
in **Silhouette Desire's** new series promotion:

The Bridal Bid

Look for
the bidding to begin
in **December 1999** with:

GOING...GOING...WED! (SD #1265)
by **Amy J. Fetzer**

And look for
THE COWBOY TAKES A BRIDE (SD#1271)
by **Cathleen Galitz** in **January 2000:**

Don't miss the next book in this series,
MARRIAGE FOR SALE (SD #1284)
by **Carol Devine**, coming in **April 2000.**

The Bridal Bid only from **Silhouette Desire.**

Available at your favorite retail outlet.

Silhouette®
Where love comes alive™

Celebrate Silhouette's 20th Anniversary

With beloved authors, exciting new miniseries and special keepsake collections, **plus** the chance to enter our 20th anniversary contest, in which one lucky reader wins the trip of a lifetime!

Take a look at who's celebrating with us:

DIANA PALMER

April 2000: SOLDIERS OF FORTUNE
May 2000 in Silhouette Romance: *Mercenary's Woman*

NORA ROBERTS

May 2000: IRISH HEARTS, the 2-in-1 keepsake collection
June 2000 in Special Edition: *Irish Rebel*

LINDA HOWARD

July 2000: MACKENZIE'S MISSION
August 2000 in Intimate Moments: *A Game of Chance*

ANNETTE BROADRICK

October 2000: a special keepsake collection, plus a brand-new title in **November 2000** in Desire

Available at your favorite retail outlet.

Where love comes alive™

EXTRA! EXTRA!

The book all your favorite authors are raving about is finally here!

The 1999 Harlequin and Silhouette coupon book.

Each page is alive with savings that can't be beat!

Getting this incredible coupon book is as easy as 1, 2, 3.

1. During the months of November and December 1999 buy any 2 Harlequin or Silhouette books.

2. Send us your name, address and 2 proofs of purchase (cash receipt) to the address below.

3. Harlequin will send you a coupon book worth $10.00 off future purchases of Harlequin or Silhouette books in 2000.

Send us 3 cash register receipts as proofs of purchase and we will send you 2 coupon books worth a total saving of $20.00 (limit of 2 coupon books per customer).

Saving money has never been this easy.

Please allow 4-6 weeks for delivery. Offer expires December 31, 1999.

I accept your offer! Please send me (a) coupon booklet(s):

Name: _____

Address: _____ City: _____

State/Prov.: _____ Zip/Postal Code: _____

Send your name and address, along with your cash register receipts as proofs of purchase, to:

In the U.S.: Harlequin Books, P.O. Box 9057, Buffalo, N.Y. 14269

In Canada: Harlequin Books, P.O. Box 622, Fort Erie, Ontario L2A 5X3

Order your books and accept this coupon offer through our web site
http://www.romance.net
Valid in U.S. and Canada only.

PHQ4994R